The
Hospitality
of the
House

Mandy O'Brien was unable to shake her premonition that she was surrounded by an atmosphere of evil. The story of her hosts, the Averys, was plausible enough—Mrs. Avery's mother, who was an invalid, needed someone to look after her between nurses, and they would all go to stay at her house for a few days.

The Averys were effusive in their cordiality toward Mandy, but they seemed to exhibit a peculiar lack of concern and sympathy for the old lady. . . .

And then, in the wake of a shocking discovery, Mandy was running—running for her life, not even sure just from what and from whom she was trying to escape.

Scene: New York State

 SUSPENSE

The
Hospitality
of the
House

Doris Miles Disney

Published for the Crime Club by

Doubleday & Company, Inc.

Garden City, New York, 1964

Library of Congress Catalog Card Number 64–11382
Copyright © 1964 by Doris Miles Disney
All Rights Reserved
Printed in the United Stated States of America
First Edition

To Liz, my daughter,
with love and appreciation
for many hours of consultation
on this book.

1

American Airlines Flight 217, five-thirty out of Boston, seven-twenty take-off from La-Guardia, headed northwest over the Catskills for Syracuse. Altitude of seventy-five hundred feet, flight time of fifty-five minutes were announced by a stewardess. Dinner was served.

The sun had set on that late August evening before the plane took off from LaGuardia, but the afterglow lingered through the first part of the flight, a panorama of gold and rose and purple that faded gradually into the darkening sky.

Mandy O'Brien, in a window seat facing west, watched it fade while she ate her dinner but was too preoccupied with the visit she was about to make to give either view or meal her full attention.

She was four months past eighteen. Whenever she had flown before, one of her parents had accompanied her. She had not admitted this to her seatmate, a pleasant, elderly man, when he asked if it was her first flight. Protecting her adult status, she had replied, "No, I've flown a few times before."

Later on, during their spasmodic conversation, she had said she was on her way to visit a friend who lived outside of Syracuse. She had not added that it was a pen pal whom she had never met or that previous plans to visit each other had been postponed from year to year for one reason or another. This time her limited reply was based on her mother's training, begun on her first trip downtown alone to go to the dentist. She was to keep all conversation with strangers at a minimum, her mother had said, and volunteer no information about herself on the bus or on any public conveyance she might have occasion to use; there were many kinds of people in the world, and those she might meet were not necessarily of good intentions. When Mandy went away to school a year later her mother had stressed again the need of reserved behavior among strangers, making a point of it until it had become a habit with the girl.

She took a paperback out of her pocketbook but instead of reading it looked out the window at the scattered lights below, which now and then converged into clusters as the plane passed over some town. Her thoughts were on Janet Avery. They had been pen pals for years, but it wasn't the same thing as meeting in person. She hoped they were going to like each other, hit it off right away. Her visit would turn out to be an awful drag if they didn't. She should have hedged on staying a whole week just in case everything didn't go well. But she was committed to it now and had to hope for the best. . . .

The public address system crackled to life. The captain announced that their flight was on time; they would land at Hancock Field in approximately ten minutes. The weather at Syracuse was clear, the temperature seventy-six.

Mandy went to the rest room and after inspecting herself in the mirror applied another touch of eye shadow above her deep blue eyes. Then she put on more lipstick, a pale coral shade that accented her summer tan, and blotted it carefully with tissues. She used no other makeup. Her fine complexion needed none. She had her hair done up in a French twist. As she smoothed it back and tightened a few hairpins, she regarded it with particular satisfaction. It was a new hair style for her; it made her look two or three years older, she thought, somewhere around twenty-one.

She had removed the box jacket of her gray summer suit. When she got back to her seat and started to take it down from the overhead rack her seatmate said, "Allow me," with old-fashioned gallantry and took it down for her.

She resumed her place and put on short white gloves. Best foot forward, she thought with a smile, to meet the Averys.

The plane banked and turned in the first phase of its smooth descent to the airport. The FASTEN SEAT BELTS sign flashed on. A stewardess moved up and down the aisle checking to see that they were fastened. The plane circled into the wind and the NO SMOKING sign lighted up. The lights on the runway seemed to come up to meet them. A moment later they skimmed past at eye level. Then the plane landed with a slight bump, slowed down and taxied to the gate where the passengers were to be discharged.

Well, here she was, Mandy thought with mingled resignation and anticipation. As she joined the crush in the aisle another thought struck her: Was she going to recognize Janet immediately from a yearbook picture taken last fall? It would be just too awkward to stand gaping at everyone. She had looked for the picture in her wallet before she left the cottage yesterday but couldn't find it and then remembered that it was in her other wallet back home in Connecticut. Maybe Janet had got out Mandy's yearbook picture, though, from Brookfield School; maybe it could all be left to her.

But no problem of recognition arose. Going down the steps from the plane she scanned the row of people waiting at the gate and picked out Janet almost immediately from her blond hair. She was still wearing it cut short on the sides and bouffant on top just as it was in her yearbook picture.

She was with an older couple—her parents, presumably— and a tall dark young man. She seemed to catch sight of Mandy at the same moment and began waving to her. Mandy waved back and quickened her step.

Standing at the gate they took stock of her. Rather tall, perhaps five seven, good carriage, slim figure, gray suit very simple but well tailored, no hat, white earrings and gloves, black pumps and large black leather pocketbook.

"She's prettier than her pictures," the other girl said. "Stunning. And just look at her suit, everything she's got on. Money, capital M."

"Jealous, Janet?" The young man smiled mockingly. "Think how you've been slaving in your father's store all summer to earn money for your new college wardrobe."

"Aren't you forgetting my week off to entertain my pen pal?" She moved away from him, edging through the crowd toward Mandy, exclaiming when they met, "Mandy! I can't believe you're here at last. And do you know, I almost didn't recognize you at first? You look so different from your yearbook picture."

Mandy laughed. "Well, so do you. I guess we've changed since they were taken. It's almost a year ago."

"I think it's your hair makes you look different," Janet said. "I adore the French twist. I must let mine grow."

"You wrote me ages ago that you were going to," Mandy reminded her.

"I know. It's just that I can't bear the growing-out bit. And Dick doesn't want me to. He says he hates that shaggy dog look. He's so bossy." She giggled. "You can't imagine all that I put up with from him."

Mandy's glance went to the dark young man smiling at her over the heads of the people around him. "Is that Dick with your parents?" she asked.

"Oh no. That's my cousin, Rollie Avery. Didn't I write you about him? Probably not. We never even knew him until just lately. He's from Wisconsin, but he's at Syracuse University this summer and he's visited us a couple of times. But let's go—" They had stopped to talk. "Mother and Dad are so anxious to meet you. Rollie says," she giggled again, "they should have brought a red carpet only there's no place to put it down."

Mandy experienced the first pinpricks of disappointment as they walked toward the gate. The giggle and the af-

fected drawl that broke out into a shrill note every so often
—Janet was nervous, of course, she was nervous herself, but
even so—

A moment later they reached the others. "Mandy, I'd like
you to meet my mother and father and my cousin Rollie,"
Janet said.

Mrs. Avery, short, rather dumpy, was effusive. She kissed
Mandy and said, "My dear, you can't imagine how much
we've been looking forward to your visit. We're simply delighted to have you here."

"Indeed we are." Mr. Avery, a big man with a broad
face, shook hands heartily. "Yes, indeed, Mandy."

"Thank you," she said. "I've been looking forward to it
too."

Rollie Avery smiled and said, "Hi, Mandy."

"Hi." She smiled back at him. He was even better-looking
close to than from a distance.

"Well, let's go," Mr. Avery said.

The three young people walked together through the tun-
nel into the lobby with the older couple ahead. Mandy
would have lingered there to window-shop the display of
gifts but Mr. Avery asked for her baggage check and led the
way to baggage claim.

They collected her suitcase, Rollie picking it up. Mrs.
Avery said, "Hadn't you better call home, Mandy? They'll
want to know that you've arrived safely."

The girl made a face. "Did my mother ask you to remind
me of it when you talked to her on the phone the other
night?"

Mrs. Avery smiled. "Well, yes, now that you mention it,
she did."

Mandy glanced at Janet and shook her head. "Wouldn't
you know it? The parents' league standing together to
watch out for their young."

"Naturally," Mrs. Avery said.

Mr. Avery dug a handful of change out of his pocket. "Why not call her right this minute, Mandy, before it slips your mind? Plenty of phones over there." He pointed to a bank of phones on the opposite wall.

"Okay." Declining his coins and taking out a handful of her own, Mandy went to a phone and made the call to Camden, Maine.

Her mother answered. Mandy said, "Well, just reporting in, Ma, that your little darling arrived safe and sound. No tall dark strangers on the plane made me any offers. There's one here, though. Janet's cousin. And is he a hunk!"

"Are you in Bentonville already?"

"No, we're still at the airport. He really is a doll."

"Who'd you say it was?"

"Janet's cousin, Ma. Rollie Avery. He came with them to meet my plane. Goes to Syracuse University."

Her mother laughed. "Well, it sounds as if the week is off to a good start. How do you like Janet?"

"Can't tell yet." Mandy spoke on a cautious note. "Just met her."

"Meaning there's already been a letdown," her mother translated. "I rather thought there would be. Your father and I were very taken with her parents, though, that time we met them. But it's Janet, of course, who matters to you."

Mandy gave a long-suffering sigh. "Ma, I didn't say I didn't like her. I just said I couldn't tell yet."

Her mother let it go. "It's only for a week, anyway," she said. "Have a good time and don't forget to offer help with household chores. You don't want to make a lot of extra work for Mrs. Avery."

"No, Ma. I'll be the perfect guest. And I hope you and Dad and your guests enjoy your cruise. What time are you starting in the morning?"

"Oh, early. We'll be back Wednesday night. Call me collect Thursday morning. Meantime, give my regards to the Averys and have fun."

"I'll do my best. 'Bye for now."

"Good-by, darling."

Mandy went back to the Averys. "Well, that's taken care of," she said. "Mother sends her regards."

"I meant to tell you to give her ours," Mrs. Avery said.

They went out of the terminal building to the parking lot. As they got into the Averys' car, a dark four-door Plymouth, Mandy asked, "How far is it to Bentonville?"

Mrs. Avery, in the front seat with her husband, turned around and said, "Janet, haven't you told Mandy we're not going to our house right away?"

"I haven't had a chance to," Janet replied.

"Well—" Mrs. Avery's glance went to Mandy. "For the next two or three days I have to take care of my mother. She lives in Noroton about seventy miles from here up Watertown way. Her health has been failing a lot this past year—she's been bedridden, in fact, since she fell and broke her hip in the yard last fall—and has had a practical nurse taking care of her. As it happens, though, the nurse is due to start on a vacation tonight and the substitute I found in Bentonville, who expected to be free yesterday, won't get off the case she's on now until Monday or Tuesday. So, in the meantime, I've got to take over myself and will need a little help from Janet occasionally."

Mrs. Avery came to a halt. She gave Mandy an apologetic smile and then said, "It's a shame it had to happen right now, just when you've come to visit us, but there's not a thing in the world I can do about it."

Mandy, startled, dismayed over arriving as a guest when there was illness in the family, exclaimed, "Oh, but why didn't you mention it to my mother, Mrs. Avery? I wouldn't have come. In fact, I needn't stay." She sat forward in the seat as if to emphasize how readily she could remove herself from the picture.

They were still in the parking lot. She looked out the window at the motel beyond it and added, "If there isn't a plane back tonight I could stay in the motel and take one in the morning. That's what my mother would want me to do. She'd be so upset if she knew that my visit was going to turn out to be a nuisance for you."

"Not at all," Mr. Avery said firmly. "Not at all. Janet's been looking forward to it all summer. And it's not as if we had to stay all week in Noroton. It's only for a couple of days and then we'll be back in Bentonville and everything will go along just the way you girls planned it. We wouldn't think of letting you turn around now and go home, would we, Janet?"

"I should say not." Janet fixed a plaintive gaze on Mandy. "I've been having fits over it. I couldn't stand going up there, Mandy, without you to keep me company. Please don't even suggest canceling out on me."

"But with your grandmother sick—"

"We only have to stay with her for a couple of days, though."

"Yes, that's right," Mrs. Avery put in. "And we'll all be there. My husband is coming too. He's taking a little time off from the store just in case I need him."

In other words, Mandy thought, Mrs. Avery's mother was dying; and here they were with a visitor, a stranger they'd never laid eyes on before, arriving in the middle of it. The week was going to be great, just great, all around.

She made further protests that were met with quick reassurances. Then another thought struck her. "I'll have to let my parents know that I'll be in Noroton in case they need to get hold of me."

"My answering service would take care of it," Mr. Avery said. "They have the Noroton phone number and they'll cover all our personal calls. I particularly told them that you were going to be our guest and to refer any calls for you to Noroton. So there's no need for you to call home again."

"Well—" Mandy let it go. She'd made enough of an issue of the whole thing already.

They drove out of the parking lot onto the access road to the airport and then took Route 11 north. It brought them to North Syracuse where Mr. Avery slowed down. "What's the name of the street where your friend lives, Rollie?" he asked.

"It's the next one on your right. But you needn't bother taking me right to the door. Just let me off at the corner. I'm only going to pick up my car and get back to my room, anyway."

"Okay." The older man pulled in to the curb at the corner and stopped.

Rollie wasn't going to the grandmother's with them. Mandy's heart sank. The one bright note in the dismal picture was being removed. But then he turned to her and said, "See you tomorrow, Mandy."

"You're coming up tomorrow?" Mr. Avery inquired. "What about your exam Monday?"

Rollie's dark eyes rested on Mandy. He said, "Oh, I'll make it. Study most of tonight, take a break tomorrow and drive back tomorrow night. After all, I can't study straight through until Monday." For Mandy's benefit he explained, "I had a language requirement to make up so I've been taking a course in French this summer. Exam scheduled for 9 A.M. Monday. Then I plan to take a well-earned rest sponging on my relatives."

Mandy, pleased that he was going to be a fellow houseguest, laughed. "Going to pass the course?"

He shrugged. "If I don't—well, *c'est la vie*." He got out of the car. "See you all tomorrow."

"Study hard, Rollie," Janet said.

Mandy caught a note of malice in her voice, wondered what it meant and then dismissed it from her mind as they drove off, leaving him on the corner with his hand raised in a good-by salute.

"I hope he is going to study hard over the weekend," Mrs. Avery remarked. "He doesn't take his education too seriously, I'm afraid."

"Oh, I'm sure he'll make out all right," Janet commented.

There was still that note of malice close to resentment. Mandy glanced at her. Her round blue eyes—china doll eyes, Mandy thought—were empty of expression as she returned the glance. Then she took a comb and mirror out of her pocketbook and began to comb her hair, tilting her head to catch the passing lights of the town.

They went on toward the next town. As they approached it Mr. Avery said, "Let's stop somewhere for a cup of coffee. It's late to ask, Mandy, but did you have dinner on the plane?"

"Yes, I did. You don't need to stop on my account."

"Well, we had an early dinner on the way down from Noroton and I could do with a bite myself. How about you, Evelyn?"

"It's all right with me," Mrs. Avery replied.

He turned off the highway at the next roadside restaurant. It was a small place nearly empty at this off-hour. Mr. Avery led them to a booth and when they were seated said, "Order me a piece of pie and a cup of coffee, Evelyn, while I make a call. There's a phone outside and I think I'd better get in touch with Jim about those refrigerators that were supposed to come in today."

He owned an electric appliance store in Bentonville and employed three clerks. That much Mandy knew about his affairs. Janet herself had worked in the store for the past two summers.

Mrs. Avery gave their order to the waitress, milk shakes for the two girls, pie and coffee for her husband and herself. Then she said, "I envy your parents going on a cruise tomorrow. It must be a lovely big boat that your father has. What kind is it?"

"It's a sixty-foot Chris-Craft."

"Last year you went to Prince Edward Island on it, didn't you?"

"Yes. It was a wonderful trip, too. I'd been wanting to go there ever since I read the Anne of Green Gables books. Did you read them, Janet?"

Janet looked blank. "I don't think so."

"The orphan girl who went to live with some people who'd wanted a boy, and who—"

"I don't read all that much," Janet said. "Not any more, I mean."

"Don't you? Well, that's a change. Remember when we were both so crazy about the Nancy Drew books? We used to write pages to each other about them."

"Oh, those things." Janet nodded languidly. "I guess I read them all."

"You certainly did," Mrs. Avery broke in with a bright smile. "You always had your nose stuck in them."

"You ought to try reading one over now, Janet," Mandy said. "I did spring vacation. It was so awful it was funny. I kept thinking of how we used to write to each other about being girl detectives when we grew up; and how I wanted to marry a man named Ned, preferably Ned Nickerson. So far, I've never even met anyone called Ned. Have you?"

"No, I haven't."

"It's a nickname for Edward but you almost never hear it used any more," Mrs. Avery said. She stood up. "I'm going to the rest room. Either of you want to?"

"No," said Janet.

"I guess not," Mandy said.

Left to themselves in the booth neither girl spoke at first. Janet opened her pocketbook—for a moment Mandy thought she was going to comb her hair again right at the table—took out a mirror and lipstick and made up her mouth. Then she studied herself complacently before she put the mirror away.

Mandy found nothing to say. She had thought that the moment she and Janet met they would be talking like mad to each other, words tumbling out of their mouths. But Janet Avery in the flesh was turning out to be different from the Janet who had been her pen pal since their mothers met at Atlantic City nine years ago and discovered that they had daughters the same age, sharing the same April 30 birthday. That first April 30, two weeks after their mothers met, they had exchanged birthday cards at their mothers' prompting. Then they had started writing to each other, keeping up the correspondence with varying degrees of faithfulness. It had sagged when they were in junior high, but when Mandy started in at Brookfield School, her first sojourn away from home, the correspondence had taken on fresh life and they had been writing to each other fairly regularly ever since. Now Mandy was here for their long projected meeting. It had almost taken place last summer when Janet was supposed to visit her in Maine but instead had ignominiously come down with mumps. They had then promised each other that this summer, come what may, they would get together.

Well, they had, Mandy reflected. But so far the visit looked like a bag.

Janet broke the short silence. "Wouldn't this Noroton deal just about kill you?" she said. "I had all kinds of plans for what we'd do in Bentonville and look what's happened! Gran has to pick this week of all weeks to have a real bad spell and the nurse has to go on vacation."

That was part of the trouble, of course. Janet was sulking because they had to go to Noroton. She'd probably had a big fight with her parents over it. Mandy didn't blame her —she'd feel the same way in her place—but still—

Mandy loved her grandmother O'Brien dearly. If she was near death— She said, "Don't stew about it, Janet. It's only a couple of days, your parents said."

"Gran's always been a pain," Janet muttered unappeased. "A real pain." She caught Mandy's surprised look and added quickly, "I know she's failing and all that, but it's not as if she was my real grandmother. She isn't. My mother's her adopted child. And she never paid much attention to me. She was too old when I came along, I guess. So I don't really care about her at all."

Mandy said doubtfully, "But if she adopted your mother that makes her your grandmother, doesn't it? Legally speaking, I mean."

"Yes, it does. At least there's that. She's got quite a lot of money although she lives like a miser. Wait till you see her house. A dump. She's way out. Like last year she sold a lot of stock and got about fifty thousand in cash for it that she hid somewhere in the house. Then she started selling her furniture and things, practically stripping the place, saying she didn't have enough to get by on." Janet shook her head. "Real nuts."

Mandy found no suitable response to make. For the next couple of days she was going to stay at the house Janet was describing, complete with its mistress, a senile, bedridden old woman.

The waitress brought their order. Mrs. Avery came back to the booth, followed a few minutes later by her husband, whose hearty friendliness Mandy thought too good to be true.

Drinking her milk shake she wished that her visit was

over and they were on their way back to Hancock Airport instead of having just left it. Or better still, that she was getting off the plane in Bangor with her parents there to meet her. They seemed all at once very far away.

2

Mr. Avery wasn't a fast driver. It was getting on toward midnight when they took a secondary road off Route 11 to Noroton. From what Mandy saw of it, going through the outskirts and then the business district, it had no particular character or distinction; it was just another small city, its population perhaps thirty to forty thousand.

She looked around her without interest. She was tired. It had been a long day since she'd got on the plane early that morning in Bangor. For the last several miles she had hardly listened to Janet's chatter about her latest beau and her plans to enter the Bentonville state teacher's college next month.

Presently Mrs. Avery said, "I think I'd better stop and phone the house, Arthur, and let Mrs. Shepard know we're on our way. We're later than we thought we'd be and she made quite a point of getting off the case as early as possible tonight."

There was a phone booth outside a gas station a block farther on. The station itself was closed. Mr. Avery turned in and parked. Mrs. Avery got out and went to the phone, came back and asked her husband for a dime.

Mandy yawned sleepily. Mr. Avery turned and smiled at her. "We'll be there soon. It's only another seven or eight miles. You must be tired."

"A little," Mandy admitted. Her gaze settled on Mrs. Avery in the phone booth. She seemed to be doing most of the talking.

"Well," she said when she returned to the car. "Mrs. Shepard sounded sort of annoyed. She expected us an hour

ago. She's supposed to pick up her husband at that restau-
ant where he works and then they're heading for their married son's in Rochester. She's just raring to get started."

"It'll be close to morning by the time they arrive," Mr.
Avery said. "You'd think they'd rather wait and start then."
He swung out of the gas station and drove a little faster
as they left Noroton behind. "You got her check ready for
her?"

"Yes, it's right here in my pocketbook."

Mandy paid no attention to this exchange. The effort to
smother another yawn brought tears to her eyes.

Beyond the built-up section of Noroton they turned onto
a narrow country road. It ran through farmland, fields and
meadows with a patch of woods now and then to relieve
the monotony. Mandy couldn't imagine what she and Janet
could do with themselves out here.

"What's your mother's name, Mrs. Avery?" she asked.

"Johnson."

"Does she live on a farm?"

"Well, it used to be one when my father was alive. No
one's worked it, though, since his death and it's been going
steadily downhill. But you can't budge my mother. It's been
her home all her married life and she says she's going to
die there. You know how old people are."

"She's quite old now?" The question seemed called for.

"Oh yes, she's well into her eighties. She and my father
were past forty when they adopted me."

"I can't remember them being anything but old," Janet
put in. "Not the kind of grandparents anyone would pick."

"Now, Janet, that's not very nice," Mrs. Avery reproved
her.

"No, but it's true. And you know what they say," Janet
giggled and nudged Mandy, "sometimes the truth hurts."

"Janet, please," Mrs. Avery said in a tone that closed the
subject. Then, addressing herself to Mandy, she said, "My

mother was in the hospital for three months after her fall but was in such a fret to come home that we had to let her. She's had a practical nurse taking care of her ever since, three or four different ones, actually. None of them will stay very long. She's not an easy patient, and on top of that, they all say the house is too isolated."

That really cooled it, Mandy thought. The house was so isolated that not even a nurse would stay there. Well, she was in for it now; she'd just have to grit her teeth and bear it for the next two or three days. After that they'd be in Bentonville, which should help some. Meanwhile, maybe Janet would improve on acquaintance. For that matter, maybe Janet was equally disappointed in her; she wasn't being too bright and gay herself tonight. Maybe tomorrow would be better.

If it wasn't, if the whole week turned out to be an utter drag, she'd just have to get through it somehow. And by this time next Saturday she'd be back home.

The car lights cut a path through the darkness that was otherwise complete around them. An occasional farmhouse indicated that people lived on this road, but they were all in darkness, their occupants apparently gone to bed for the night. There were no street lights to lessen Mandy's feeling of being out in the middle of nowhere. There were just the fields and meadows unrolling in front of them and being left behind. Then she saw lights ahead in a house set far back from the road. Grandma Johnson's, no doubt, she thought wryly. It was isolated all right—with the nearest neighbor half a mile back on the road. No wonder the nurses wouldn't stay.

"Well, here we are," Mr. Avery said briskly, slowing down to make the turn onto a rutted gravel driveway with weeds and grass sprouting from it. The house, picked up by the car lights, was tall and narrow, drab from lack of paint, the last coat applied so long ago that it had weathered to

no color Mandy could name. It reared up from the feature-
less landscape, a graceless box with a porch tacked on at the
front and a tangle of evergreens and overgrown shrubbery spreading out on the left and blocking off the side yard
from view. The lawn had been cut recently but still had a
look of neglect with seedling oaks scattered over it, off-
spring of parent oaks whose branches rose above the roof.

On the other side of the house the driveway ran in a
straight line to a dilapidated barn and outbuildings in back
of it. A tan Volkswagen was parked near the barn. The
nurse's car, Mandy thought.

The house was larger than it had seemed at first glance.
A two-story ell attached at the rear added to its size, although it lacked the attic or crawl space that gave greater
height to the main structure.

A dim light burned upstairs in the ell and a brighter
light in the room below it. The downstairs room was the
kitchen with a door standing open on the back or side
porch. Light streaming out the door conveyed no sense of
welcome to Mandy as she got out of the car and looked
around her. The whole effect was one of desolation and
decay, of a house stranded and forgotten and sinking into
ruin.

She went up the sagging porch steps with Janet. Mr.
Avery, carrying her suitcase, walked in back of them while
his wife hurried ahead, saying over her shoulder, "Excuse
me, Mandy, I'm going to run right upstairs to check on my
mother and send the nurse on her way."

She paused at the kitchen door. "Arthur, I think you'd
better take Mandy's suitcase up the front stairs. If Mother's
asleep we don't want to all go tramping through the ell."

"Okay," Mr. Avery said.

Janet held the door and Mandy preceded her into the
kitchen, which took up the first floor of the ell except for an
enclosed stairway along the rear wall. An ancient electric

range and refrigerator and a wooden table and chairs in
need of paint made up the furnishings. The wallpaper was
dark with age, the linoleum worn bare in spots. Janet hadn't
exaggerated when she called her grandmother a miser.
She lived like this with fifty thousand cash hidden somewhere in the house.

"This way," Mr. Avery said, opening a door in the front
wall of the kitchen.

It led into a dining room with dark varnished woodwork
and old-fashioned oak furniture, the telephone on the sideboard the one modern touch. A cloth was spread—the
Averys apparently ate at least their main meal of the day at
the claw-footed table—but other than that, Mandy wondered how long it had been since anyone had sat down at it.
The room smelled musty with age and disuse.

They went on into the living room. Its furnishings were
as old and out-of-date as those in the dining room, and
shabbier-looking. The wallpaper was faded and the rug
threadbare. A wide-open window on the front porch
couldn't overcome the musty smell. The whole house,
Mandy thought, smelled as if Janet's grandmother hadn't
let any air in on herself in a long time.

Old people, it seemed, minded drafts; all but her own
grandmother O'Brien. She was as brisk and alert as a girl.
But then, she was much younger than the old lady upstairs,
not seventy yet.

Mandy hoped that in another ten years she wouldn't shut
herself up in her house and live among shabby relics of the
past.

The living room led into a center hall through an open
archway that had once been fitted with double doors, a
companion set, probably, to the double doors closed on a
room across the hall. The varnished oak stairway went up
along the opposite wall. On Mandy's left was the front door
with stained-glass side lights. A massive hallstand took up

the wall space beside it. On her right the hall went back to
the kitchen, the open door revealing the sink and a cupboard beyond it, reflected brightly in the hallstand mirror.
Except for that one bright area the hall was dark and
gloomy, the only light coming from one bulb in an overhead
fixture.

Mr. Avery carried Mandy's suitcase upstairs, the two girls
following him. At the head of the stairs the door to the
ell stood ajar, giving Mandy a glimpse of a narrow corridor
that ran its full length, dimly lighted by a single bulb at its
far end where the back stairs came up.

The old lady's room must open off the corridor, Mandy
thought, hearing voices from that direction, one of them
Mrs. Avery's, another, deeper voice, presumably the nurse's,
and then a high, quavery voice that must be Grandma
Johnson's, awake after all, and making some sort of complaint.

There were several rooms opening off the upstairs hall.
One of the two front bedrooms had been assigned to
Mandy. It had no wall switch. Mr. Avery went into the
room and pulled the cord on the center light. It consisted of
a bulb with a frosted glass shade suspended on a chain
from the ceiling. The wiring in the house, the girl reflected,
dated back to Thomas Edison's youth. She couldn't think
when she'd seen anything like it; to say nothing of the old
lady's thrift in the use of low-watt bulbs. Aside from the
kitchen there didn't seem to be an adequate light in the
house. Or perhaps it was to cover up other deficiencies that
the lights were so poor, she thought next as she looked
around her room.

It was uncompromisingly square and bleak. The floor was
covered with frayed straw matting; the furniture, bed,
bureau and washstand were of funereal black walnut. Two
chairs, a straight-backed one in front of one window, a
rocker in front of the other, didn't match the rest of the

furniture. There were no lamps; the ceiling fixture was the only light in the room, which had the same musty smell as the others, although both windows were open.

"Here you are," Mr. Avery said, setting her suitcase on the straight chair. "Come downstairs when you're ready and we'll all have a nightcap."

He went out of the room leaving the door ajar. Mandy heard footsteps on the back stairs and then Mrs. Avery's voice muffled by distance calling out, "Have a nice trip now," and a reply that she didn't catch. A moment later the back door closed and a car started in the yard. She looked out the side window and saw the Volkswagen leaving.

"There goes the nurse," she said to Janet.

"Yes. And we're stuck here until the new nurse comes."

"Oh well, it's just for a couple of days," Mandy said, playing the polite guest. She opened her suitcase. "Might as well get this over with." And then, making conversation, "Which room is yours, Janet?"

"I'm next door to you. Mother and Dad have the front room across the hall and Rollie will have the little room next to the bathroom when he comes." After a pause Janet added, "I was hoping we could share a room, but Gran doesn't have any twin beds and Mother said we were both so used to sleeping alone we wouldn't get any rest sleeping together in one of the double beds."

"I guess that's right," Mandy said. She opened the closet door. It had no center pole, just hooks with wire hangers on them.

Janet said apologetically, "This house is like out of Noah's Ark. Nothing like our house in Bentonville. We'll be together in my room there. I have twin beds and we can talk all night if we want to."

"That'll be fun." Busy with her suitcase, Mandy tried to sound enthusiastic.

After being away at school for four years she was an

efficient packer and unpacker. In a few minutes her big suitcase stood empty in the closet, blouses, skirts and dresses were hung up, shoes arranged in a neat line on the closet floor, toiletries spread out on the bureau, sweaters, underwear and accessories placed in the bureau drawers.

While she was unpacking, Janet, very much in the way, stood in front of the mottled mirror fussing with her hair and studying herself absorbedly.

Mandy put her hostess presents, a gold tie clasp for Mr. Avery, a pin set with cultured pearls for Mrs. Avery and a wide silver bracelet for Janet, on the bed.

Janet squealed with delight when she opened her box. "Oh, Mandy, it's stunning, just stunning," she exclaimed, putting it on and holding up her arm to admire it. "Thanks a lot. Let's go downstairs so I can show it to Mother and Dad."

"I'm glad you like it," Mandy said. She picked up her gifts for Mr. and Mrs. Avery and went downstairs with Janet.

Mr. Avery was in the living room settled in front of the portable TV with a drink.

"We brought that along," Janet said. "Gran doesn't even have one. Just a radio in her bedroom. Imagine, in this day and age."

Mandy made no comment. She conceded to herself that the other girl's criticism of her grandmother might be due to embarrassment over the way she lived, but it was getting to be awkward for Mandy, who didn't know what reply to make to it.

"Your mother will be down in a minute," Mr. Avery said to Janet. "Then we'll all have a drink together to celebrate your pen pal's arrival." He beamed at Mandy. "How about it? Do your parents let you have one now and then?"

"Yes, occasionally," she replied, not adding that it had

happened only twice and that it didn't matter anyway because, while she liked beer, she didn't like liquor at all.

"Well, it's legal in New York State at eighteen so you and Janet are under the wire," Mr. Avery said. "You're going to Skidmore this fall, aren't you? Any drinking you do there will be strictly legal too."

"The college kids I know don't seem to worry much about whether it's legal or not," Mandy told him.

He got to his feet, moving lightly for so big and heavy a man. "I've got some Seagram's V.O. out there. Janet has hers with water, but what about you, Mandy? Water or club soda?"

"Soda, please." She looked at Janet who had settled herself on the sofa. Her pen pal, she thought, probably did more drinking than she ever admitted to her parents or, for that matter, in letters to Mandy. When you were eighteen, if you were just starting to have an occasional highball, you weren't apt to like the taste of liquor well enough to drink it with plain water.

Mrs. Avery, who had come down the back stairs, put in her appearance.

"Well, Gran's gone back to sleep," she announced. "Her sleeping pills are nearly all gone, though. I'll have to ask Dr. Cramer for a new prescription."

"Let's hope she doesn't wake everybody up in the middle of the night," Janet said. "Like the way she made a pest of herself last night."

"Janet, I want you to stop that kind of talk," Mrs. Avery said sharply. "You'll have Mandy thinking you're pretty hardhearted about your poor grandmother."

Mandy already thought that. Janet's indifferent "Sorry" made no impression on her.

Mrs. Avery turned a saccharine smile on Mandy. "Don't mind her, dear. It's just her way of talking."

What kind of an answer did the older woman expect to that? The mother was as bad as the daughter.

Mr. Avery came in with their drinks on a tray. After he had passed them around the girl presented her gifts to him and his wife. They were opened and duly admired. Mrs. Avery brought in a plate of crackers and cheese.

Presently Mandy got to her feet, glass in hand, and wandered around the room and then out into the hall. She had been taking only small sips of her drink, finding it much too strong, but there wasn't, as in movies, a convenient potted plant on which she could get rid of it. She opened the screen door and went out on the porch. A moment later she had poured most of the drink over the railing.

The others followed her out. There were folding chairs. "It's nice and cool out here," Mrs. Avery said. "I hope you don't mind that the house seems a little close, Mandy. Mother's kept it shut up for years."

A white lie seemed called for. "I hadn't noticed," the girl said.

"Old people get like that," Mr. Avery remarked. "Anyone like another drink?"

"No, thank you," Mandy said.

He made fresh drinks for his wife and Janet and himself. Mandy noticed that Janet tossed hers off with practiced ease.

A gaunt old tiger cat suddenly appeared on the steps.

"Is that your mother's cat, Mrs. Avery?" Mandy asked.

"No, it's a stray. It's been hanging around for the past couple of days."

The girl was a cat lover. She moved toward it holding out her hand and making coaxing sounds. The cat let her get almost within reach of it and then fled.

"Oh, the poor thing," she said. "It's terribly thin. Couldn't we give it something to eat?"

"No indeed, we'd never get rid of it then." Mrs. Avery

spoke firmly. "My mother doesn't like cats. We mustn't encourage it."

Mr. Avery looked at his watch in the light that came
from the living room window. "It's one o'clock," he announced. "Time for bed, Evelyn. You going to sleep on the
cot in your mother's room?"

His wife stood up. "I'll see how she is. Girls, I don't want
you to sit up half the night talking. Don't forget, Janet,
Mandy's been traveling all day."

Nothing could have appealed to Mandy less than a late
talkfest with the other girl. She gave her a smile of apology
and said, "If you don't mind, Janet, I'd just as soon go
straight to bed myself. I'm dead and I'll have to go to Mass
tomorrow. Incidentally, do you know where the nearest
Catholic church is?"

Janet looked at a loss for a moment and then glanced at
Mrs. Avery, who said quickly, "There's a new one right on
our side of town. I'll call in the morning and check the time.
What Mass do you want to go to?"

"The last one. Eleven, probably."

"I'll ask about it. I'm sure Janet would like to go with
you, wouldn't you, dear?"

"Yes, I'll go," Janet replied without noticeable enthusiasm.

"I'm afraid we're terrible heathen ourselves," Mrs. Avery
added. "Christmas and Easter are about our speed."

Mandy couldn't recall what church the Averys belonged
to.

Good nights were said. The two girls went upstairs ahead
of their elders.

"Why don't you use the bathroom first," Janet suggested.
"I've got to set my hair. Mother put out clean towels and a
washcloth for you. The blue ones on the bar over the tub."

Mandy undressed quickly, picked up her toothbrush and
toothpaste and went into the bathroom.

From its size it must once have been a small bedroom or sewing room. It had a huge tub standing high off the floor on claw feet, a stately object that looked curiously naked to Mandy's eye. It took her a moment to realize that this was because it had no shower above it, no shower rail or curtain; it stood, in fact, completely clear of the wall.

She eyed it with dismay. She liked showers, not tub baths. Well, she thought, reaching for the blue washcloth, it was just one more stupid setback in what looked like a whole week of them.

Her bed turned out to be another setback, with a lumpy mattress that sagged in the middle. She was used to falling asleep almost as soon as her head hit the pillow, but tonight she was wakeful, twisting and turning in a vain effort to make herself comfortable and finally getting out of bed to look out the front window. There were no lights of any kind, no neighboring houses, just nothingness.

She thought about the Averys, Mr. Avery too hearty to be true, Mrs. Avery too gushing, too much inclined to take command of all conversation. Janet herself? Well, she was a great disappointment so far; silly giggle, empty china doll eyes, shallow conversation, self-centered indifference to her dying grandmother, everything about her, including her preoccupation with her looks, rubbed Mandy the wrong way.

Was there nothing she liked about Janet? Standing at the window, she couldn't think of a thing, could only wonder how they'd remained pen pals all these years.

In letters, of course, the giggle, the empty-eyed look hadn't come through. In letters Janet hadn't been constantly admiring herself in mirrors or found occasion to make slighting remarks about her grandmother. In passing references to the old lady, she hadn't considered her broken hip or failing health worthy of mention. That was the kind of person she was, very different from the impression she gave of herself in letters. It was disillusioning; it was too bad they'd ever met.

At last, with a sigh, Mandy went back to bed, comforting herself with the thought that at least Rollie Avery would be around tomorrow. He would take some of the pall off everything.

3

Janet awakened her with a knock on her door the next morning. Entering the room she said, "Mother called St. Joseph's. There's an eleven o'clock Mass. It's after nine-thirty so we thought you'd better get up."

She was wearing frilly pink baby doll pajamas and a matching robe. Her hair was still on rollers; she had slept with them on. "The bathroom's all yours," she said.

The sun was shining. A bluejay skimmed past the window as Mandy looked out. Her room seemed less bleak in the cheerful morning light. She got out of bed and while she was getting into her robe told herself that perhaps, after all, something could be salvaged from her visit, which had looked so unpromising last night.

Janet turned to go. "I'll get dressed and start our breakfast," she said in her languid drawl. "I'm afraid there's not much hot water. Mother told me to be sure and leave enough for you but I forgot."

Mandy pushed away the thought that naturally Janet would think only of herself. Not even a tub bath in water barely lukewarm, not even having to scrub off the ring Janet had left on the tub could disturb her determination to make the best of the situation.

The day promised to be hot. She put on a sleeveless cotton dress. Then, remembering her mother's admonitions on the duties of a guest, she made her bed and tidied her room. When she had assembled clean white gloves, her missal, pocketbook and a scarf to substitute for a hat, she was ready to go downstairs.

Janet's door was open. Her bed was still unmade, her clothes strewn all over the room. Mandy felt virtuous.

Mrs. Avery, wearing a neat housedress, was outside in front of the house picking a bouquet of flowers from a neglected border. Mandy gave her a friendly good morning through the screen door and went on to the kitchen.

The kitchen door stood open. As she went past it Mr. Avery came out of the barn and padlocked the door. From its tumbledown look, she wondered what there could be in the barn that was worth locking up.

Janet had set two places at the kitchen table and was frying eggs at the ancient electric range. Mandy, offering to help, poured juice and made toast.

They had just sat down at the table when a cry came from upstairs over their heads.

"My grandmother," said Janet.

"Hadn't you better see what she wants? Your mother's outside," Mandy told her.

"I suppose so." The other girl got to her feet.

The cry came again. "Evelyn! Janet! Somebody help me."

Janet, without undue haste, opened the door to the back stairs and shouted, "All right, I'm coming."

Mandy heard the footsteps overhead, her voice, not at all gentle, then the older voice, cracked with age.

When Janet came back downstairs she said, "She couldn't find her handkerchief. That's what all the yelling was about. She's completely off her rocker today."

She resumed her place at the table and picked up her fork. A moment later she complained, "My damn egg's cold. It's that old bitch's fault."

Mandy was shocked, but didn't let herself show it. "How is your grandmother today?" she inquired.

"I didn't ask. The doctor's coming, I guess. Mother told her you were here so I said I'd take you up to meet her later on."

Mandy looked at her watch. It was ten twenty-five. "How long will it take us to get to church?"

"Oh, maybe fifteen minutes."

Mrs. Avery came in the kitchen door carrying the flowers she had picked. "Aren't they lovely?" she said. "I'll find a vase for them. Janet, have you looked in on Gran?"

"I was just up there."

"She seems worse this morning. I wish the doctor would hurry up and get here." She ran water in the sink and set the flowers in it. "Hadn't you girls better get started? Don't forget a hat, Janet."

"Mandy's got a scarf. I'll wear one too."

Mr. Avery came in wiping his hands on his shirt. "I just gave the car a quick wash," he said. "Can't have you girls going to church in a dirty car, no siree. You look as pretty as those flowers, the pair of you."

"Don't they, though," his wife agreed. "One blond and one dark. I hope they come home to us, Arthur. We don't want any Noroton boys running off with them, do we?"

Mandy found this remark so inane that it made her uncomfortable. Janet, on her way upstairs to get a scarf, seemed not to mind or perhaps wasn't listening.

"You really do look just lovely, Mandy," Mrs. Avery continued. "That blue dress matches your eyes. Irish blue eyes, aren't they?"

"I suppose so," the girl said.

She was glad to escape from Mrs. Avery's excessive flattery when Janet came downstairs. The car key was in the ignition. Janet backed the car around and headed down the driveway.

In the bright sunlight the grass looked fresh and green all the way to the road. In back of the house there was a field reaching to a patch of woods. On either side the fields were marked off by a rail fence that was falling apart. But even on this sunny August morning there was nothing of interest in their surroundings, Mandy thought. Just the forlorn-looking house rearing up out of the fields with a narrow country road in front of it.

She wondered how old Mrs. Johnson had stood the loneliness of her life since her husband's death. Apparently she had no car; a telephone was her only link with the outer world.

Eleven o'clock Mass was crowded. On the way out of church Mandy noticed two good-looking boys eyeing them and murmured to Janet, "Couple of interesting males across the aisle. Do you know them?"

Janet glanced their way and shook her head. "No, I don't."

That was that.

But there was Rollie, Mandy reminded herself. Noroton couldn't be written off as a complete desert when he was going to be around.

He had already arrived. His car, a black Renault Dauphine, was in the yard when they got back to the house. The cat was also present, although only Mandy noticed it sticking its head around the corner of the barn. But again it fled at her approach.

Rollie came out onto the back porch to greet them. Her spirits went up a notch at the sight of him. "Well, hi," she said. "How'd the studying go? You must have stayed up all night to get here so soon."

He shook his head. "At three o'clock this morning I'd had it. I set my alarm for seven and racked out. I studied for a couple of hours after I got up, then took off for here. I thought we could go for a swim at Watson's Pond and after dinner I'd go back to the salt mines."

"You poor overworked guy," Janet said and once again Mandy caught an edge of malice in her voice. There was some undercurrent of feeling between these two that she couldn't define.

They went into the big sunny kitchen that was, for all its shabbiness, the pleasantest room in the house.

Mr. Avery was sitting at the table reading the Syracuse *Post-Standard* with a can of beer in front of him. He looked up at Mandy. "Did you say a prayer for an old sinner?"

"If you're talking about yourself, I didn't know you needed one," she replied lightly.

Mrs. Avery came down the back stairs. "Gran's gone to sleep since the doctor was here," she remarked to no one in particular.

"Oh, he's been?" Mandy said.

"Yes, not long ago. You must have passed him on the road. He wasn't very encouraging about her condition. He says she's failed just since he saw her yesterday."

"Well, she's pretty old, Evelyn," Mr. Avery put in. "You've got to expect that she'll go any time."

"She's had a long life," Rollie said. He went to the refrigerator and got out a can of beer. "Anyone else care for one?" he asked.

"I'll have one," Mandy said sitting down opposite Mr. Avery at the kitchen table. Janet dropped down on a chair near the door, took out her comb and began to comb her hair.

At least she wasn't combing it at the table, Mandy thought.

Mrs. Avery opened the refrigerator and took out a tray of ice cubes. "It's a little early in the day but I think I could do with a drink," she said.

"Make me one too," Janet said.

"Now really, dear, you're a little young to start having a drink in the morning," the older woman protested.

Janet's gaze rested on her steadily. "Make me one, Mother. Let's say because it's Sunday."

"Oh well . . ." Mrs. Avery made them both drinks.

Mandy felt a little troubled by the general attitude of

the group. She tried to tell herself that it wouldn't help the old woman dying upstairs if they all sat around with long faces, but Rollie and Mr. Avery arguing cheerfully about the Yankees, Mrs. Avery asking on a brightly interested note if Janet had seen anyone they knew in church, Janet saying no as she finished off her drink—it all seemed callous to the girl. No one expressed any real concern for Grandma Johnson; they were simply waiting for her to die, and somehow conveying the impression that the waiting was a nuisance, a bore. Mrs. Avery was only an adopted daughter, it was true, and Mandy had no personal knowledge of how people usually acted in the face of imminent death, but the behavior she was witnessing seemed off-key to her in some fashion that she couldn't put her finger on, more involved than it should be if lack of affection for the old lady were the only factor.

It wasn't, of course. Somewhere in the house she had hidden fifty thousand dollars in cash. It opened up all sorts of unpleasant possibilities.

Mandy closed her mind to them, picked up the comic section of the newspaper and began to read it.

Janet set her empty glass on the drainboard. "Gee, it's getting hot," she said. "Let's go for a swim. You brought a suit, didn't you, Mandy?"

"Yes, I brought one."

"Let her finish her beer," Rollie said.

"Well, I'll get my suit on." As Janet drifted off toward the back stairs Mrs. Avery said, "Look in on Gran and see if she wants anything."

"Uh-huh."

The house had old flooring that gave away every sound. Mandy listened to the other girl's footsteps going straight through the ell without stopping at the old lady's room. Mrs. Avery, who had picked up a section of the paper herself, seemed unaware of this dereliction.

There was no sound at all from overhead. The old lady, so ill that the doctor was making daily visits and finding her worse each day, might have died up there alone in the last few minutes for all that her family knew.

It gave Mandy the fidgets. She couldn't pay attention to Dick Tracy. At last she said, "Your mother must be asleep, Mrs. Avery."

"She should be after her medicine." The older woman went on reading for a moment and then became aware of the implications of Mandy's remark. She got up, went out into the front hall and called, "Janet, is Gran asleep?"

"Yes, she is," Janet called back.

But she hadn't been near her grandmother.

She came downstairs a few minutes later in a Kelly green one-piece suit. She had, Mandy conceded to herself, a beautiful figure. A little too much bosom perhaps—or was that cattiness because Mandy knew that she was a bit skimpy herself in that department? No, a second glance told her, she wasn't just being catty. Janet was a trifle too lush all over, too wide in the bottom, calves slightly thick, a round little bulge at the waistline. Either she hadn't told the truth when she wrote early in the summer that she'd lost seven pounds or else she'd gained it all back since.

Mandy enjoyed a moment of feeling smug about her own sleek lines and then laughed at herself inwardly. Janet in a bathing suit could hold her own with any girl.

"Hey, you two, get your suits on," she said.

Rollie looked up from the sports pages and said, "Won't take me a minute. You go ahead, Mandy."

The girl went out into the hall and up the front stairs. She had been closer, sitting at the kitchen table, to the back stairs but no one suggested that she use them. They seemed to be reserved for Mrs. Avery and Janet in attendance on the old lady's needs. It would probably disturb her to have people going back and forth in the corridor past her door.

Mandy had forgotten her momentarily but in the upstairs hall stopped to listen at the corridor door. There wasn't a sound. The old lady must be asleep.

It turned out that she wasn't. While the girl was getting into her black wool suit she heard her calling, "Evelyn, come up here. Evelyn!" and then heard Mrs. Avery hurrying up the back stairs.

Perhaps she'd been too quick to judge Janet's mother. She couldn't be expected to spend every waking moment with the old lady.

Mandy met Rollie at the foot of the stairs on his way up. He stepped back against the double doors to let her pass but she came to a halt and asked, "Is there another living room in there?"

"I think Grandma Johnson calls it her parlor. But would you rather have it a mystery?" his voice took on a teasing note. "We could call it Bluebeard's chamber."

"Bodies all over the place?" Mandy fell in with his tone.

"Well, shall we look?" He slid back the doors and said, "No bodies."

"None at all?" She looked into the room over his shoulder. It was dark as a cave, shades drawn to the sill, the musty smell so strong that she wrinkled her nose against it. There was no rug on the floor and very little furniture. The only attention the old lady could have given the room in years was when she had sold the rest of the furnishings.

It was depressing to think about. Mandy was relieved when Rollie closed the doors.

4

They went to Watson's Pond in Rollie's Renault, the three of them crowded together on the front seat, following a dirt road that lay a little beyond the house. The pond, fringed here and there with trees, was less than half a mile long and about a quarter of a mile wide. It had what passed for a strip of beach on the far side but most of it was surrounded by a grassy bank sloping down to the water. The beach was already occupied by a group of youngsters; Rollie and the two girls spread their towels on the grass across the pond from them and stretched out to sunbathe.

After twenty minutes or so of this Mandy found the sun too hot and climbed down the bank into the water. It was a little muddy but felt cool and fresh as she swam out to the middle of the pond.

Rollie followed her in, an excellent swimmer, better than she was, although she had won medals at school. He was like a seal, swimming on the bottom, turning somersaults, pulling her under with him, executing flawless dives from a log. They ducked each other and raced back and forth across the pond, Mandy laughing and breathless, enjoying herself more than at any time since she had got off the plane.

Janet finally came in to join them but proved to be an indifferent swimmer, more concerned about not getting her hair wet than with sharing their fun.

After she went back up the bank there came a moment when it wasn't fun for Mandy. Rollie pushed her down and held her under with his foot, close enough to shore for his head to be above water. She experienced blind panic, a sensation of bursting lungs, and struggled frantically until she was free and floating to the surface to gulp in air.

He was laughing. "What was the big idea?" she blazed at him. "It's not so funny to scare people."

"Did I scare you? I'm sorry. I was just fooling."

"You fool a little rough," she retorted.

He apologized again. Janet, in an irritated voice, called from the bank, "Rollie, cut it out, whatever you're doing."

It was building up into a small scene. Mandy didn't want that. She forced a laugh and said, "It's okay, it's nothing, Janet," and swam out into the pond.

But Rollie had spoiled the first pleasant interlude of her visit. He had a cruel streak; he had meant to frighten her. She would regard him with a more critical eye hereafter.

More people had arrived at the pond including two or three boys who were Mandy's age and ready to display interest in her. But Janet, as with the pair at church that morning, professed not to know them.

Rollie had followed Mandy out of the water and said to her with an air of reproach, "So you're looking other guys over when I'm around? I don't go for that."

"Too bad," she said.

"Don't forget, I'll be back tomorrow," he continued. "I guess I'd better pin you down right now to go to the drive-in with me tomorrow night. Okay?"

"Yes, but—" She broke off, not wanting to ask in front of Janet if she were included in the invitation. Then she said, "Well, let's wait and see."

Janet, lying face down on her towel, said nothing.

Mandy began to dry her hair and then combed it. It reached below her shoulders, gleaming richly in the sunlight.

Rollie watched her comb her hair. She was lovely, he thought, letting his glance travel over her. That sleek, greyhound spareness she had was as provocative in its fashion as Janet's blatant curves.

Presently he got to his feet. "I put a few cans of beer in the car," he said. "They'd go good right now."

"You probably forgot an opener." Janet propped herself up on one elbow and gave him an acid glance.

"No, I didn't. Come on, Mandy, keep me company." He reached down a hand and pulled her to her feet.

On the way to the car she asked, "Are you going to invite Janet to go to the drive-in too?"

He raised his eyebrows. "Haven't you heard that three's a crowd?"

"But I'd feel funny about going out and leaving her home. After all, I'm her guest."

"She won't mind. After she's dragged you out here in the sticks she's got no right to expect you to sit around and hold her hand."

"Doesn't she know any boys around here so that we could double?"

"I suppose she knew some when she was a kid, but I doubt that she's kept in touch with them. She hates this place. From what she's said, she hardly ever comes up here to see her grandmother any more."

They reached the car parked at the side of the road. The beer was in an insulated bag in the back. Rollie took it out and got a can opener from the glove compartment.

As they started back to the pond he said, "Don't worry about Janet. You'll be out of here in a couple of days and she knows plenty of guys in Bentonville, including the famous Dick."

"What's he like, Rollie?"

"All right, I guess, if you go for the meathead type."

That was encouraging, Mandy reflected. He'd have meathead friends that Janet would be fixing her up with.

She was sitting up when they got back to her, hands

clasped around her legs, chin resting on her knees, face sullen. "I thought maybe I'd die of thirst before you brought the beer," she said.

"Knock it off," Rollie said. "We were only gone five minutes."

He opened a can of beer and gave it to her. She complained that it was warm. This wasn't so, but Janet would have found fault with it, Mandy thought, if it had just come out of the refrigerator. She was in a snit about something. Not being asked to go to the drive-in? If that were the case, Mandy wouldn't go herself. It didn't matter; she wasn't so keen on going out with Rollie since he had frightened her in the water.

Janet was still sulking on the way home and after they arrived went straight upstairs to change, leaving Mandy on the front porch with Mr. and Mrs. Avery. Rollie went up next and must have said something to bring her out of her mood; by the time she came down her manner was pleasant as she asked Mandy to excuse her while she helped her mother get dinner on the table.

When Rollie came downstairs Mandy went up to her room to change.

Her hair was still damp. After she had put on a blouse and shorts she pulled it back into a ponytail. A cry, half moan, half whimper, brought her up short as she opened her bedroom door and went out into the hall. The cry came again. She hesitated, eyeing the door into the ell. Should she see if there was anything she could do for the old lady? No, she couldn't intrude on her when they hadn't even met each other yet. She'd better get Mrs. Avery.

She hurried downstairs and out into the kitchen. Janet was setting the dining room table. Mrs. Avery was at the sink slicing a cucumber into a salad bowl. She greeted Mandy cheerfully. "I'll bet you're starved," she said. "There's nothing like a swim to give you an appetite."

"I think your mother needs you," the girl said. "She was sort of moaning when I came downstairs."

"Oh. Well, I'd better see what's the matter." Mrs. Avery put down the paring knife and cucumber and turned toward the back stairs.

Mandy picked up the knife, sliced the rest of the cucumber into the salad bowl and then the radishes and tomatoes that were set out on the drainboard. She listened to the sounds overhead, a querulous wail, Mrs. Avery's voice firm and commanding as she moved back and forth, and presently silence.

Somehow the silence, coming so suddenly, was more disturbing than the wail. Janet, carrying plates into the dining room, paid no attention.

Mandy poured dressing over the salad and began to toss it.

Mrs. Avery came down the back stairs. "I gave her another pill," she announced. "She'll sleep for hours now. Oh, you've got the salad made. Thank you, Mandy. I'll call my husband to slice the ham. I don't think she'll last much longer."

Her tone was almost brisk. She might have been referring to a change in the weather. It took the girl a moment to realize that she meant the old lady was going to die soon.

She went out to the front porch to summon her husband. A moment later he came trailing after her into the kitchen. "Let's get on with it," he said. "I could eat a horse myself. Where's the carving knife, Evelyn? The game's going to start in another half hour."

Mrs. Avery looked at Mandy, laughed and shook her head. "I could be lying dead here on the floor and if they had a baseball game on TV that husband of mine would step right over my body to watch it."

Mandy made no reply. How could Mrs. Avery joke about death with her mother dying upstairs? And yet she did; the awesome fact seemed not to trouble her or any of the others. Janet, who had finished setting the table, was giggling in the living room over something Rollie had said. Mr. Avery, slicing the ham, reminisced in a jovial vein about the amateur baseball he had played in his younger days. None of them showed the least sign of sorrow or regret that a life close to theirs was coming to an end.

But no matter how little the old lady really meant to them, they should allow her some dignity in her dying; she shouldn't be given sedatives constantly just so that she'd be less trouble to take care of.

Well, maybe it wasn't quite fair to look at it that way. The doctor paid her daily visits; he must know what was going on.

But suppose he didn't?

This was a startling thought with implications so far-reaching that she thrust it quickly out of her mind. She was dealing with perfectly ordinary people; not people she could warm to or like, but perfectly ordinary people.

"There," Mr. Avery said stepping back from the table and picking up the platter of ham. "Let's go."

It occurred to Mandy as she followed him into the dining room that there'd been no mention of the old lady's dinner. She had been given a pill that would make her sleep for hours but she hadn't been fed first.

When they were all seated at the table with Rollie and Mr. Avery taking up their discussion of the Yankees where they had left off earlier, and Mrs. Avery pressing food on everyone, Mandy found herself still thinking about the old lady's lack of dinner. Perhaps she was too near the end for solid food, but shouldn't she have soup, milk, some sort of nourishment to keep her going?

The girl tried to tell herself that it was none of her business but finally, against her better judgment, asked, "Is your mother able to eat at all now, Mrs. Avery?"

The older woman looked taken aback for a moment. Then annoyance flickered across her face. She said with some stiffness, "She couldn't eat a meal such as we're having, Mandy, and I don't try to keep her on our schedule. But she had soup and tea and fruit just before you came back from swimming. She'll have another light meal when she wakes up."

It so happened that this exchange took place during a pause in the discussion being carried on by Rollie and Mr. Avery. They both looked at her, Janet, too, as if they were aware of the note of criticism her question contained.

She blushed hotly and dropped her gaze to her plate. What did she know about the care of a dying person? She should have kept her presumptuous thought to herself. Wasn't there enough going wrong on this visit without her opening her mouth and putting her foot in it?

But no more was said about Grandma Johnson. Mrs. Avery asked Mandy if she'd done much shopping yet for college clothes. The girl seized gratefully on the change of subject. Janet entered into the conversation and the uncomfortable moment was left behind.

When dinner was over Rollie announced that he'd better get started for Syracuse. He said good-by to the Averys, then reached for Mandy's hand and said, "How about walking out to the car with me and wishing me luck tomorrow?"

She walked outside with him. "What time is your exam?" she inquired.

"Nine o'clock."

"So you'll be finished by eleven?"

"Come on, you don't think it will take a genius like me the whole two hours?"

They went around the corner of the house. The cat was crouched in the yard beside Rollie's car.

He stopped short. "There's that goddamn cat again."

Before Mandy even realized his intent he picked up a

stone, hurled it at the cat and hit it on its side. With a screech of pain and fright it streaked off around the barn and out of sight.

"Well," she said. "What was that all about?"

"I can't stand cats. Particularly that one. Night before last it was yowling under my window half the night. Just let me get my hands on it and I'll wring its neck."

His tone, his clenched jaw told her that he meant what he said. He would kill the poor cat if he got hold of it.

Mandy's face, so easily read, made her feelings plain to him. He gave her a hard stare. "So I don't like cats. Is that a crime?"

She looked back at him levelly. "Does that mean you have to stone them or threaten their lives?"

"If they stay away from me, I stay away from them. But this one's got under my skin and now I've given it fair warning to keep its distance."

"Let's forget it," Mandy said.

"Okay." He smiled suddenly, charmingly. With conscious charm, she thought, turned on like a faucet labeled boy-dazzles-girl smile.

"You haven't wished me luck yet," he reminded her.

"Well, lots of it."

"Thanks." He opened the door and got into his car. "See you tomorrow and don't forget we're going to the drive-in tomorrow night."

He started the motor, waved and drove away.

She watched him go without regret. Like everything else around here Rollie was no loss.

5

Janet was waiting for her on the porch. "Let's go for a ride," she said.

"Fine. But shouldn't we help your mother with the dishes first?"

"She doesn't mind doing them. And if I don't get away from this hole I'll go stir crazy."

Janet was back in her nasty mood. She had been in and out of it for hours, ever since they had gone swimming at Watson's Pond, in fact. Whatever it was, maybe she wanted to talk about it.

On the way to the car Mandy caught a glimpse of the cat peering around the barn. From its behavior, it hadn't always been a stray. It was probably hungry and hung around here looking to people for food. The first chance she had she'd sneak something out of the refrigerator for it. But that might not be such a good idea. If she encouraged it to stay around and Rollie got his hands on the poor animal he would kill it. It had better not yowl under his window tomorrow night.

It dawned on her then, belatedly, that Rollie had stayed here Friday night, the night before her own arrival. That was odd. With all the studying he talked about, why spend hours driving out from Syracuse Friday, going back Saturday and returning again for a few hours today? If he'd brought his books and spent the whole weekend it would have made more sense.

Getting into the car she started to ask Janet about it but checked herself. Whatever was eating Janet seemed to be connected with Rollie and she'd better not mention him. It was none of her business anyway if he wanted to spend the last two days shuttling back and forth between here and Syracuse.

Janet backed the car around and when they reached the road turned right on it away from Noroton.

"Where are we going?" Mandy asked, making conversation.

The other girl shrugged. "Who cares? We're out of the house. That's all that matters to me."

They rode in silence for an interval, Mandy making no further effort to talk but looking around her at expanses of farmland spreading out on either side as far as the eye could see. She was used to the much smaller scale of Connecticut farms with their limited boundaries of fence and stone wall and wood lot. What she was looking at now was wider horizons, reaches of land rich with grain and orchards and produce with fine herds of cattle grazing in pastures. Her grandmother O'Brien, who had grown up in western New York, would be interested in it, she thought.

Janet finally broke the silence. "Light me a cigarette, will you?" she said. "They're in my bag."

The straw bag lay on the seat between them. Mandy took out a cigarette and lighted it for her.

"Thanks." Janet took it from her. "You don't smoke much, do you?"

"Some. But there was always such a fuss if we got caught smoking in our rooms at school that it was hardly worth the trouble."

"I've been smoking for six or seven years now."

"Janet! You started when you were twelve? I didn't know that."

Janet shot a quick glance at her. "Don't you say a word about it in front of my mother."

"Of course not. But why didn't you ever mention it in your letters?"

The other girl giggled. "There's a lot of things I never put in writing. Probably some of them would surprise you."

"Would they?" Mandy didn't press the matter. At least Janet seemed to be coming out of her sulky mood.

The road took them to a village and eventually to a state park on Lake Ontario. Two boys tried to pick them up on the beach but Janet snubbed them thoroughly, somewhat to Mandy's disappointment since the taller one, who had showed interest in her, was real cute, she thought.

Janet, explaining her sudden burst of propriety, said that her mother would have a fit if it ever came out that she'd picked up a strange boy at a beach; her father would get huffy about letting her take the car again; and besides, she'd promised Dick she wouldn't cheat on him, wouldn't look at another boy while she was in Noroton.

She was too voluble. Mandy didn't believe a word of it. Janet knew as well as she did that flirting at a beach was just meant to be fun and needn't lead to anything. She had another reason for snubbing the two boys. But Mandy made no comment on it. She would stick to her resolve to be the perfect guest and eventually it would be Saturday. . . .

They stopped for hamburgers on the way home and arrived just before dark. When they drew near the house, stark in its solitude, Mandy felt that their respite from it had ended much too soon.

They found Mr. Avery watching TV. He got up and turned down the volume when they came into the room.

"Where's Mother?" Janet inquired.

"Upstairs giving your grandmother some supper."

Mandy thought there was challenge in the glance he flicked at her; but perhaps she only imagined it because of the embarrassment she had suffered at the dinner table.

A moment later he seemed amiable enough as he said to

her, "I guess your father keeps pretty busy this time of year."

"Yes, he does. He's been away most of the summer."

"Building a road somewhere?"

"Two of them, I think, here and there."

"Imagine doing that. Going all over the country building roads and bridges, it's really something." Mr. Avery shook his head and laughed ruefully. "Makes my electric appliance business look like pretty small potatoes."

"Oh, I don't know about that." Mandy made her tone vague.

Mrs. Avery called from upstairs, "Janet?"

"Yes, Mother?"

"Just checking that you're home." She went back into the ell.

"Is Mrs. Johnson any better?" Mandy asked Mr. Avery.

"Well, more rational my wife says. She remembered that Janet brought a friend here and wanted to know what your name was."

Janet said, "Maybe this would be a good time to take you up to meet her, Mandy. She'll keep harping on it until we get it over with."

"Okay." Mandy, getting up from her chair, half wanted and half didn't want to meet Janet's grandmother. It would give her a chance to see for herself what the old lady was like and how well looked after she seemed to be; but on the other hand, it was probably going to be very difficult to find anything at all to say to her.

Janet led the way upstairs. The ell corridor was as dimly lighted as the night before with the one bulb at the far end turned on. In daytime the window opposite the bedroom door would make it much brighter. It seemed strange that the Averys, now that they were in charge of the house, didn't buy a few decent light bulbs. But perhaps they were so used to the poor lighting that it didn't occur to them to change it.

"Does your grandmother have just one big room here in the ell?" Mandy asked.

"Well, it's over the kitchen and used to be the same size," Janet replied. "But when Gran took in her invalid sister— she's dead now—some years ago, she had part of the room sectioned off to make a little entry and lavatory."

She opened the corridor door as she spoke. It opened into the entry with the lavatory beyond it. Another door on their right led into the bedroom. Low moans, broken by mumbles, came from it.

"My God." Janet gave an exasperated sigh. "Sounds like Gran's off again." She rapped lightly on the door and said in a loud whisper, "Mother?"

Mandy stood back against the opposite wall beside a small table that held a telephone and a shaded lamp pushed aside to make room for a tray. The old lady's supper tray, she thought, taking inventory of a plate with bits of egg and toast on it, an empty teacup and custard dish.

Mrs. Avery opened the bedroom door and stuck her head out, finger to her lips. "No use trying to have Mandy meet her tonight," she whispered. "She was fine a little while ago but now she's all confused again."

"Who's there?" The old voice from the bedroom sounded sharp and fretful to Mandy but not particularly confused. "I want my supper. I'm hungry. Give me my supper right this minute."

Mrs. Avery glanced at Mandy and said in an undertone, "Her mind wanders so. She's just had her supper and she's forgotten it already. You'll have to meet her some other time. Janet, will you take the tray down with you?"

"I'm hungry," the fretful voice from the bedroom reiterated. "I want my supper."

"All right, Mother," Mrs. Avery said soothingly, stepping back into the room and closing the door.

"Isn't that just too bad, Mandy," Janet muttered picking up the tray. "You don't get to meet Gran tonight."

Mandy made no reply. They went back along the corridor into the upstairs hall. Janet came to a halt. "Mind taking down the tray?" she asked. "I've got to go to the john."

"All right." Mandy took the tray from her and went downstairs and out into the kitchen with it.

She set it on the drainboard, started to turn away, then paused for a second look at it. The egg on the plate—she touched it tentatively with her forefinger—had a glazed crust. The bits of toast, the custard left in the dish were hard and dry. This wasn't the old lady's supper tray. It wasn't the lunch tray of soup, tea and fruit Mrs. Avery had mentioned at the dinner table.

Breakfast tray? It had to be, even though the custard seemed out of place. Was breakfast the only meal they'd given the old lady all day?

"I'm hungry," she had complained. "I want my supper."

What were they doing, trying to starve her to death?

That was fantastic. It couldn't be true.

Couldn't it? If they cared nothing for her, if she had become a burden, if they wanted her money?

Her money. Fifty thousand in cash hidden somewhere in the house. They certainly wouldn't try to hasten her death until they had found it.

But what if Janet had lied when she said it hadn't been found or hadn't been told by her parents that they had found it?

Then there'd be no further need to keep the old lady alive.

Mandy went slowly into the living room where Mr. Avery was watching a movie on TV. She sat down and pretended to watch it too, although her mind was going around in circles. She didn't know what to make of the tray. Her first reaction to it, murder by starvation, seemed, on second thought, wildly melodramatic.

Mrs. Avery hadn't said that it was the old lady's supper tray. If she'd just been fed it was perfectly possible that her supper tray was still in the bedroom and that the one Mandy had brought down had been left standing there all day.

How many trays did they have for her? Surely more than one; the old lady had been bedridden for months. There might very well be several trays in use.

Mandy began to feel better. It must be this gloomy old house that sent her imagination on such rampages. The Averys were just ordinary, everyday people.

But still, for extra reassurance, it wouldn't hurt to go out into the kitchen when Mrs. Avery came downstairs and see for herself if she was carrying another tray.

Janet appeared first and sat down beside Mandy on the sofa to show her the new hairdo she'd found in a magazine. Between that and the TV going, the girl didn't hear Mrs. Avery come down the back stairs. By the time she became aware of her in the kitchen and went out to get a glass of water, it was too late to check on trays. The older woman was already on her way into the living room and said, "Well, Gran's asleep at last and I've done her dishes. Now I'll ask my husband to make us all a drink."

Mr. Avery made drinks. They took them out on the porch and again Mandy managed to get rid of most of hers sitting on the railing with her glass tilted over the shrubbery.

Mrs. Avery took charge of the conversation, talking enthusiastically about the many plans Janet had made for Mandy when they got back to Bentonville.

Her enthusiasm seemed forced, artificial to the girl. Why did she make the effort?

Later on in bed, as wakeful as the night before, Mandy came to the conclusion that Mrs. Avery's manner was a cover-up for some different feeling that she didn't want to reveal. There was something funny about it, about all three of them; little things kept cropping up that didn't seem quite right—or was it the atmosphere of the old house again affecting her judgment?

She wondered next what the Avery's would be like back in their own surroundings, the big, comfortable-looking white frame house of the snapshot Janet had sent her years ago with her parents standing on the front steps. The snapshot had long vanished but Mandy remembered the house. It was situated on a residential street with near neighbors and, presumably, street lights, a sense of life and activity. The Averys would seem different, perfectly normal, in their own home. This house was like a tomb, especially at night when darkness closed in on it.

Tomb. Murder by starvation. She was having pleasant thoughts tonight. And all because she found herself marooned in a dreary old farmhouse out in the country. Not her first one, either. She had been in others like it in Maine.

No, she hadn't. None quite like this one. There was something about it, not just its derelict state and isolation, that made her uneasy. It came—the thought sprang unbidden to her mind—from the ell.

Was it the imminence of the old lady's death in that bedroom? Not necessarily.

The supper tray? No, the Averys couldn't be withholding food from her. When Mandy had thought about it earlier she had overlooked the fact that the doctor came every day, to say nothing of the nurse who had been in attendance until last night.

But there was something going on connected with the old lady and the ell; if not starvation, something else; something odd, something almost goosefleshy. . . .

Now, Mandy thought, she was moving into the realm of instinctual knowledge, feeling or whatever. But there it was. It couldn't be explained away.

6

Bright sunshine Monday morning brought some change in her nighttime mood, but it was less marked than yesterday's. A residue of unanswered questions about the Averys and the old lady lingered in her mind and a faint sense of uneasiness kept them company.

The house was quiet. No one had awakened her. Janet's bedroom door was still closed when she emerged from her room and took possession of the bathroom. Her watch showed nine o'clock.

She was leisurely over her bath. Janet hadn't used up the hot water this morning.

On her way back to her room she encountered Mrs. Avery, who came out of the ell with a tray in her hands, the same one Mandy had carried downstairs last night. Almost automatically the girl ran her eye over the empty juice glass on it, the cup and saucer, the plate with a crust of toast. The old lady had been given her breakfast, as much, probably, as she could be expected to eat.

"How is your mother this morning, Mrs. Avery? Did she have a good night?"

"You didn't hear me up with her?"

"No."

"Well, I'm glad of that. I tried to be quiet as a mouse. Her hip seemed to be bothering her, the one she broke last fall. The doctor's going to have to give her more pain pills, I'm afraid."

"Oh. I suppose there must be some sort of dope in them to keep her comfortable." Mandy made her tone casual.

"Yes, I should think so. But she has to have them. I had to give her an extra one at four o'clock this morning. She didn't wake up after that until a little while ago when I brought up her breakfast." Mrs. Avery gave a deep sigh and shook her head. "These are sad days for me. But no use dwelling on it."

She set the tray on the newel-post and knocked on Janet's door. "Come on, dear," she called. "It's after nine o'clock, time for sleepyheads to be up."

It was a sickening sweet little act, Mandy thought. And somehow phony, as phony as Mrs. Avery's performance a moment ago in the role of dutiful, worried daughter. What was she, anyway, a woman who had been playing different parts all her life because her real self had never pleased her?

"Janet!"

There were groans and protests from behind the door, but Mrs. Avery was firm. "Mandy's up. I'll get your breakfast started."

"Don't get her up on my account," the girl protested. "She doesn't have to entertain me every minute."

But Janet was announcing that she was awake. They heard her get out of bed.

"Well, that's that." Mrs. Avery picked up the tray and turned toward the stairs. "Which would you prefer, Mandy, toast or English muffins?"

"Muffins, please." The girl watched her descend the stairs. She had been too insistent that Janet get out of bed as soon as Mandy was up. It created the impression that she couldn't be left to her own resources at all; that she needed an attendant—or was it a guardian?—every waking moment.

There was her imagination getting busy again at the very start of the day. All right, give it free rein. Were they keeping her away from the old lady? If they proposed another visit to her and it didn't work out, perhaps Mandy could manage to go into the ell on her own to see what the old lady's condition actually was; it wouldn't be a nice thing to do but perhaps the situation called for it.

Not now, though. Janet opened her bedroom door and stood yawning in the doorway. She had on her frilly pink baby doll pajamas. Her eyes were smeared with yesterday's makeup and her hair, matted from being teased, stood up around her face. A ray of sunlight shining through Mandy's open door picked out a darker line at her scalp. Janet, who had always maintained in her letters that she was a natural blonde, needed a retouch.

They said good morning to each other. Janet moved toward the bathroom and Mandy went on to her room. She looked at herself in the mottled mirror, feeling fresh and clean compared to the other girl who hadn't even washed her face before she went to bed last night, who had too overblown an appearance in her frilly pajamas. She would not again be envious of Janet's curves.

She got dressed and then made her bed before she went downstairs.

Janet came down while Mrs. Avery was scrambling eggs and Mandy toasting the muffins. Her pink housecoat was a little dingy, but she had washed her face and brushed her hair.

They sat down to breakfast. "Where's Mr. Avery this morning?" Mandy inquired.

"He had to run in to the drugstore to renew one of my mother's prescriptions." Mrs. Avery poured herself a cup of coffee and sat down with them. "I didn't have my grocery list made out when he left, Janet. I thought you girls might go in and do the shopping after he gets back."

Mandy gave Janet a mischievous glance across the table and said, "By car or dumbwaiter?"

"What?" Janet looked at her blankly.

"Don't tell me you've forgotten already? I wrote you the whole story last fall."

"Oh yes." But Janet's giggle came halfheartedly.

"What is all this about a dumbwaiter?" Mrs. Avery asked.

"Oh, there was one in the dorm at school that went down to the kitchen and Debbie, my roommate, who's quite small, was able to get into it. We'd lower her at night to swipe things to eat and then have a party in our room. We had a real thing going until the housemother caught Debbie one night and we were all campused for a week." Mandy spoke quickly wanting to be done with the story. It had fallen flat. Self-centered Janet had forgotten all about it.

Mrs. Avery, on the other hand, plied Mandy with questions as to what had gone on and laughed harder than the silly little story warranted. But it was all pretense; it was a case of like mother, like daughter.

The girl found herself studying the pair. Mrs. Avery showed more friendliness than Janet, but it was only skin-deep. They both had cold hearts. There was none of the closeness between them that should exist between a mother and her only daughter and that did exist between Mandy and her mother in spite of the head-on collisions they sometimes had. These two, in the basic sense of what their relationship should be, were more like two strangers thrown together in passing.

She didn't know which one she liked less.

A car came up the driveway. Mrs. Avery hurried to the door to see who was arriving.

"Is it Rollie?" Janet asked.

"Of course not. How could it be so early? I thought it might be the doctor, but it's your father."

He came in to the kitchen door carrying a bottle wrapped in white paper. "Here's Gran's prescription," he said handing it to his wife. "Doctor been yet?"

"No." Mrs. Avery passed the bottle on to Janet. "Take it upstairs, dear. If Gran's awake give her a teaspoonful. If she's sleeping just leave it on her bureau. And get dressed while you're up there so that you can go to the store."

"Yes, Mother." Janet went up the back stairs. Her bare feet made a padding sound in the corridor overhead. Then Mandy heard a door open and realized that she was listening for it, that she had fallen into the habit of listening to every sound from the ell. Grandma Johnson's self-appointed protector, that's what she was.

Protecting her from what?

From being deprived of food that might prolong her life. Or, more likely, from a figment of Mandy's own imagination based on not one solid, provable fact.

Thus the girl argued with an instinct partly visceral, older than reason, that told her there was something wrong with this house, its whole atmosphere and its occupants.

She helped Mrs. Avery clear the table and then wandered over to the door. She saw Mr. Avery, who had gone outside, standing near the padlocked barn door with his head bent as if in deep thought. As soon as he caught sight of Mandy, though, he straightened up and came back to the house. When he was seated at the table with a cup of coffee his fulsome smile indicated that he hadn't a care in the world. "Well, young lady, how are you this beautiful morning?" he inquired.

"Fine, just fine." Leaning on the back of a chair Mandy retrieved him from the limbo of friend's parent and for the first time really examined his appearance.

He had a broad reddish face, bulbous nose and heavy jaw. His eyes, light gray or blue, were small and restless, darting here and there, flickering over her face and away as if some unease in him kept them on the move.

He lighted a cigarette and then tore the matchbook cover into shreds, rolling them up with thick, blunt-tipped fingers.

Mrs. Avery, running water into the dishpan, talked with excessive brightness about what a lovely day it was. The girls must go to the pond for a swim, she said; if they'd just do the grocery shopping for her, she'd take care of everything here. And so forth.

Mandy's glance went from one to the other in cool appraisal. What was bugging them, anyway?

The phone rang. Mrs. Avery went into the dining room to answer it.

Mandy heard her say, "Oh, good morning, Doctor. . . . No, not too good. . . . Oh, I see. Well, thank you for calling."

She hung up and returned to the kitchen. "Dr. Cramer," she said. "He's late starting on his rounds this morning and didn't want me to worry in case he didn't get here until afternoon. It was nice of him to let me know."

"Has he been your mother's doctor very long?" Mandy asked.

"Oh yes, for years. He's quite elderly now himself. About ready to retire, I guess."

Elderly. Not so sharp, probably, as he once was; not so quick to notice everything about his patients.

Mandy gave herself a mental shake. She'd better stop this right now before she turned into a real weirdo.

But a moment later when Mr. Avery started teasing her about Rollie having his mind on her that morning instead of his exam, her thoughts again took an errant path. Only a fragment of Mr. Avery's attention was being given to what he said; the rest was devoted to something else, some problem he couldn't stop thinking about.

She hadn't noticed before that he had a mean look in his eyes. And when he wasn't smiling—did he smile so much because he knew it served as a disguise?—his mouth was brutal.

Smile, heartiness, genial voice, all were phony. He was phony, like his wife, like Janet.

What a pen pal she'd picked—or rather, her mother had

picked for her—when she was an eager-beaver fourth-grader.

All she wanted from the whole family was out.

Mrs. Avery started washing the dishes. Mandy picked up a dish towel and dried them over her protests that it wasn't necessary.

Janet came downstairs in a dressy sleeveless blouse, short shorts and red straw sandals. She didn't even have good taste in clothes. Everything she wore was too fluffy, too bright or clashed with something else.

Mr. Avery gave her a twenty dollar bill and Mrs. Avery handed her the store list. Mandy was expected to keep her company. A drive into town for the groceries was her treat for the day, she reflected dryly, going out to the car.

It was too bad she didn't look forward more to Rollie's arrival and their date that night. But his behavior yesterday had put her off; for all his striking good looks and the charm he could exert when he chose to, she didn't really like him any better than the rest of the family.

It didn't take them long to do the shopping at an outlying supermarket. Mrs. Avery's grocery list was, in fact, rather sketchy. Mandy took heart from it. It indicated that they weren't going to be in Noroton much longer.

But then, as they were leaving the market, she found herself wondering why the list hadn't included a few delicacies, something interesting to tempt the old lady's appetite—or was that the very last thing Mrs. Avery wanted?

She sighed resignedly. She was back on that subject again. Trying to curb her imagination was a waste of time. She might just as well not worry about letting it run as wild as it pleased.

Janet was prepared to go back to the house now that the shopping was done, but Mandy, to postpone their return, said, "Let's stop somewhere for a Coke."

"Well . . . all right." Janet swung the car toward the cen-

ter of town and found a place to park in front of a big drugstore.

They sat down in a booth with their Cokes and looked
around. Two girls in a booth across the way were displaying
an elaborate lack of interest in a group of boys at the soda
fountain who were talking about somebody's basketball record and paying no attention to them.

"The high school hangout," Mandy said. "I'll bet you
thought it was wonderful to come here a few years ago."

"Except that my father was usually with me." Janet giggled. "Imagine trying to make any time with him around."

"But did that matter?" Mandy smiled in reminiscence.
"Whenever I went anywhere like this even if no one knew
I was alive I'd make myself think they did and put on a
bored, aloof air and enjoy every minute of it."

"Really?" Janet shook her head. "I wouldn't get any kicks
out of that."

"But don't you see?—I was posing for my own benefit.
I'd tell myself that any boys who were around were dying to
get to know me and all the other girls were madly jealous
while I—" Mandy broke off as Janet took her mirror and
lipstick out of her pocketbook and began to make up her
mouth.

"Gee, I look a mess this morning," she said.

It was hopeless to try to carry on a conversation with her.

They finished their Cokes and left, Mandy stopping on
the way out to buy a postcard to send her grandmother.
She bought none for her parents; she would be in touch
with them by phone before a card could reach them.

Outside the drugstore her glance fell on an interstate
bus sign in front of a tobacco shop across the street. A sudden wave of homesickness swept over her. If she could just
walk across the street and buy a ticket for the next bus
heading east—

There was nothing to stop her. She had her pocketbook

along with an ample supply of money in it provided by her parents in case an emergency arose while she was out of touch with them and far from home.

Well, from her point of view an emergency had arisen. She couldn't stand the Averys, father, mother, daughter or cousin Rollie. Her visit—was it actually less than forty-eight hours ago that she'd got off the plane in Syracuse?—had turned out to be a colossal flop. Or something worse than that, considering the old lady and the house itself.

The house was a horrible place. Almost—well, almost frightening.

Frightening. It was an adjective she had used countless times casually, exaggeratedly. Wasn't she using it that way now? Of course. But still—

There was nothing in the world to stop her from crossing the street to the bus station to wait for the next bus east. She could tell Janet she'd just remembered something that meant she had to be back in Maine by tomorrow and that Janet must say good-by to her parents for her and send on her things at her own convenience.

There was nothing in the world to keep Mandy from doing this except for one thing that was as potent in restraining her as physical force would have been. It was the fear of making a fool of herself; of looking like a baby running home to mama from some formless bogeyman.

She got into the car and closed the door. Janet started the motor and turned back toward the house.

7

They found Mrs. Avery looking solemn on their arrival. "The doctor's been here," she announced. "I guess he thought he shouldn't wait until afternoon to see Gran. He says she's lost still more ground. There's nothing much that can be done about it, he says, except to try to keep her comfortable."

"Oh, that's too bad," Mandy said and then, snatching at the chance to escape, "It's too much for you to have a houseguest around at a time like this, Mrs. Avery. I'll get packed and leave today. I can stay in Bangor with my grandmother until my parents get home. I know my mother will think it was an imposition that you've had me on your hands at all. She'll say that as soon as I found out about your mother I should have turned right around and taken the next plane home."

"Why, Mandy, you mustn't even mention such a thing," the older woman protested. "We're delighted to have you and you're no trouble at all. Janet would be lost out here away from all her friends if she didn't have you. Isn't that right, dear?"

"Yes, it is," Janet said. "I'd just about die of boredom on my own."

"I'm sorry, but I really mustn't stay," Mandy said. "There's a bus station in Noroton where I could get a bus to Syracuse and then see about a plane."

"What's this, what's this?" Mr. Avery came into the kitchen from the front of the house. "Do I hear you talking about leaving, young lady?" He added with mock plaintiveness, "What's the matter, don't you like us any more?"

Mandy couldn't answer him truthfully; she could only

reiterate that with a serious illness in the family they shouldn't be burdened with a guest.

"I don't blame you to want to leave," Janet put in poutingly. "Stuck out here a million miles from nowhere."

"Oh, that's not it at all," Mandy said for politeness' sake.

But Mrs. Avery looked hurt and was voluble in apologies to Mandy for having had to bring her there at all. Mr. Avery inserted his apologies and somehow it seemed to become the old lady's fault that she had picked that particular week to start dying—or perhaps it was the nurse's fault for going on vacation just then.

The girl found the situation more and more embarrassing. She was no match for the Averys; she ended up assuring them that she didn't mind staying out here in the country and that her chief concern was over being underfoot at a time when they shouldn't have the bother of a guest.

Mrs. Avery was quick to insist that she was no bother at all; that they actually needed her to keep their spirits up.

"Yes, indeed," Mr. Avery said. "You're doing us a favor by staying, Mandy."

"And tomorrow is the last day we'll be here," Mrs. Avery added. "I called the nurse in Bentonville while you were gone. She goes off the case she's on now at seven tomorrow night. I told her that we'd pick her up at her house about nine o'clock and drive her up here. First thing Wednesday morning we'll leave for Bentonville. I'll have to be back and forth, of course, to keep an eye on things here, but in the meantime, I'll get you settled at our house. So you see," she smiled eagerly at Mandy, "there's no need for any more talk about your leaving us. I feel bad enough as it is over the way your visit's gone so far."

The door to escape closed. Mrs. Avery began to put away the groceries. She said presently, "I'll make a salad and some sandwiches and we'll have an early lunch. Then you girls can go over to Watson's Pond for a swim. Rollie will probably arrive before you're back." She shook her finger playfully at Mandy. "Wild horses couldn't keep him away knowing you're here."

The girl merely gave her a neutral smile.

At lunch Mrs. Avery was even chattier than usual as if to cover up with small talk the lack of other entertainment for their guest. Toward the end of the meal she started to talk about theatrical experiences of her youth.

"Oh, were you an actress?" Mandy was interested. "Janet never told me."

"Well, Little Theater." Mrs. Avery laughed self-deprecatingly. "I doubt that I could have aspired to anything else."

"I guess you couldn't," Janet scoffed.

"I don't know about that." Mr. Avery came to his wife's defense. "I thought your mother was pretty good, times I saw her on the stage."

She'd probably been awful, Mandy thought. Her artificial manner must date back to those days.

Mr. Avery had finished his lunch. He pushed back his chair and got to his feet. "Guess I'll go in on the couch and have me a little siesta," he said.

Mandy's gaze followed him as he left the kitchen with ponderous tread. He might as well be back home in Bentonville for all the good he did his wife here, she reflected. But perhaps she wanted him on hand for the moment of her mother's death. No, that couldn't be the reason; he was going back to Bentonville Wednesday.

Mrs. Avery's flow of reminiscence continued; the time she'd started to serve food to her stage family and discovered that props had neglected to put plates on the table; the time her leading man was so self-conscious that they bumped noses when they were supposed to kiss. "Like we were Eskimos," she added gaily.

Mandy laughed and said to Janet, "Remember when I

wrote you a few years ago that at last I'd found out what people did with noses when they kissed?"

"I remember." Janet giggled. "But I don't think the problem ever bothered me."

"It did too. You've forgotten. We wrote to each other about it a couple of times."

"Well, at least we don't have any trouble nowadays with noses, do we?" Janet leered at Mandy and rolled up her eyes. "I should say not."

Mandy smiled briefly and dropped the subject. Janet's attitude robbed it of its humor.

They did the lunch dishes together while Mrs. Avery fixed soup and crackers and juice on a tray—the same tray as last night and this morning, Mandy noticed—and took it upstairs.

She was still in the ell—apparently involved in some sort of an argument with the old lady, to judge from their voices—when the girls went up to get into their bathing suits.

Mandy was ready first and downstairs ahead of Janet. She had the kitchen to herself and when she saw the cat outside took advantage of the interlude to see what the refrigerator offered for it. Cold cuts were nearest to hand. She unwrapped a couple of slices and slipped out the kitchen door with them.

The cat scurried off at her approach. She dropped the cold cuts in front of the barn and returned to the house. Looking back over her shoulder she saw the cat move forward warily. A moment later it devoured the cold cuts in a few gulps.

The poor thing was starved, she thought. It had been someone's pet. It was funny that it stayed around this one house out in the country so far away from other houses. It acted as if it belonged here.

But the Averys said it didn't. They said old Mrs. Johnson

didn't like cats. Why, then, had it picked out this house? Cats were apt to be as attached to places as to people but here it received no food or shelter or attention.

She went back into the kitchen and was still pondering the matter when Janet, trailing a towel over her shoulder, came into the room and said, "Ready? Let's go."

They spent most of the afternoon at the pond. A few children were splashing around across from them but no one else appeared.

"Why do you suppose more people don't come here?" Mandy asked.

"I guess they mostly go to a little lake—I forget what it's called, it's an Indian name—on the other side of Noroton."

"Oh. Maybe we should try it." There would be more life at the lake. Mandy was surprised that Janet hadn't headed for it before this.

"It's nearer to come here. I don't like to go too far away in case my mother needs me to help her with Gran."

Janet's explanation, cloaked in sudden daughterly solicitude for Mrs. Avery, didn't make sense to Mandy. They would be no more out of touch with Janet's mother at the lake than they were in the hours they spent here at the pond. But it wasn't for her to point this out.

A little later she swam by herself. Janet, not wanting to get her hair wet, didn't go into the water. She had brought along a manicure set and spent considerable time doing her nails.

The afternoon dragged. Except for desultory conversation about clothes, they found little to say to each other. Mandy sought a common meeting ground by bringing up incidents they'd written to each other about in the past but Janet wasn't interested.

Rollie hadn't arrived yet when they got back to the house. Mr. Avery was reading a magazine on the front porch; his wife was in the kitchen starting dinner.

The two girls went upstairs. Mandy, unlike Janet, spent no time in narcissistic study of herself in front of the mirror and was dressed well ahead of the other girl. She picked up the paperback mystery she had been reading on the plane and went downstairs.

Mr. Avery was still on the front porch. After she had talked with him for a minute or two she made her way around the tangle of evergreens on the side lawn to the grape arbor in back of the house. There was a rickety bench in the arbor. She stretched out on it to read.

Presently she heard a car come up the driveway. Rollie? Probably. She made no move to go and greet him. She was enjoying her respite from the Averys.

But then she found them intruding themselves through the plot of her book, based upon the projected murder of a rich old man who had a family eager to inherit from him. Mandy couldn't help being reminded of Grandma Johnson. She was an old lady who had money and a family waiting for her to die. There was a major difference between the fictional old man and the real-life old lady, though. Her family wasn't plotting her murder. They were merely waiting, in varying stages of boredom and impatience, for her to die a natural death.

There were lots of people, no doubt, who felt the same way about elderly relatives; it just happened to be the first time she had ever come in contact with it. Naturally it made her uneasy and prone to dream up all sorts of things, including murder plots that had no place outside of fiction.

The house didn't help, either. Its shadowy depths, its isolation and decay would encourage Poe-like imaginings in anyone.

Nor was she alone in how she felt about it. Janet, who had been coming here all her life, hated the place; her mother, who had once called it home, made constant apologies for it.

The old lady who owned it was apparently the only person who found no fault with it. She and the house had gone downhill together, their best years behind them.

But had the house ever had best years? Lying on her stomach, chin propped in her hand, Mandy looked at it squarely, trying to visualize it as a well-kept farmhouse in Grandma Johnson's younger days. But all she could see was its present state of abandonment and desolation, of a house unloved and untended for many a year.

But not sinister; not the setting for a plot to murder an old lady who clung to life too long to suit her family. Just a derelict old house.

Resolutely she turned her attention back to her book and had read a whole page before Rollie and Janet furnished an interruption. She heard them talking and then saw them, glimpsed them, actually, through the thick matted leaves of the grapevine as they skirted a shed in back of the house, headed in her direction.

She didn't want their company. Then, before she could make up her mind to disclose her presence, the tones of their voices told her they were quarreling.

They stopped short facing each other. "Don't try to tell me that," Janet said sharply. "You're laying it on pretty thick, aren't you?"

"I've got to make it look good, baby. You know that as well as I do."

"That good?"

"My God," Rollie exclaimed. "If there's one thing I can't take, it's jealous women. Lay off it, will you?"

"Oh sure. Have it all your way. But just remember, I'm not guaranteeing how well I'll keep on taking it."

"Oh, for Chrissake—" He caught her by the shoulders and gave her a hard shake. A moment later, with Mandy peering at them in astonishment through the vine, they were locked in a tight embrace, kissing each other passionately.

It was Rollie who broke it off. He let Janet go and stepped back from her. "That wasn't very smart of us," he said. "We'd better go find Mandy. Where'd she get to?"

"Front porch, I guess. She came downstairs before I did."

Mandy started to jump to her feet. It would be too humiliating if they caught her eavesdropping. She'd just die.

But the grape arbor, open at both ends, offered no hiding place. The only thing she could think of to do was to put her head down on the bench and pretend to be asleep.

She lay still and listened. They were making small talk now, Rollie telling Janet how much cooler it was here than in Syracuse, the direction from which their voices came indicating that they weren't coming toward her but were cutting across the lawn. She opened one eye to follow their progress. They didn't look back or they would have seen her.

The moment they went around the barrier of evergreens out of her sight she scrambled to her feet and ran out of the arbor by the back way. She ran past the shed and other outbuildings and darted behind the barn. She told herself that she must look an utter idiot running and hiding like this, but it didn't matter. Anything was better than letting Rollie and Janet know she had been in the arbor.

There wasn't time yet to think about the meaning of what had gone on between them. She had to get farther away before they came looking for her.

The barn screened her from the house as she ran across the field in back of it. A stone wall, falling into ruins, bordered the far side of the field. It was a respectable distance away from the scene of her eavesdropping. She sat down on it.

8

When Rollie and Janet appeared at the edge of the field a few minutes later Mandy waved to them, presenting the picture of a girl idly sunning herself on an old wall.

"Hey, what are you doing away over there?" Rollie called to her.

"Just took a walk, that's all," she called back to him.

He and Janet sauntered across the field to her. "We didn't know what had become of you," he said dropping down on the wall beside her.

"Oh, I did a little reading, too." She had taken her book with her when she ran out of the arbor and held it up for his inspection. "How'd your exam go?"

"Rougher than I expected."

"Think you passed?"

"We'll see." His dark eyes rested on her caressingly. He moved his hand along the wall to cover hers, smiling with the charm that he turned on and off. "How'd the day go for you, baby, away out here in Grandma's gulch?" he asked.

She was on his left. Janet, who had sat down on his right, was ignored. All his attention was for Mandy. It was hard to believe that the scene she had witnessed from the grape arbor had actually taken place. Janet had nothing to say. She stared morosely into space while he gave her an exaggerated version, almost a caricature, of the fifth wheel treatment.

No wonder she had reproached him for laying it on pretty thick. It was perfectly clear now that she had meant his playing up to Mandy. He had said he had to make it look good but at the moment he was doing more than that; using Mandy as his weapon, he was punishing Janet for her display of jealousy. Mandy herself was supposed to be reduced to mooning delight by attention paid to her.

She was furious but had to hide it. She couldn't show a sudden change of attitude that might start him wondering what had brought it about.

Keeping up her end of the conversation, she asked herself what was going on between these two. They were in love with each other—or at least Janet was in love with Rollie—but couldn't let it out in the open. They were, after all, cousins, the relationship close enough for Janet's parents to object, and therefore in need of a smoke screen like Mandy.

She was the real fifth wheel, not Janet, who had a claim on him. There had been something about the way they embraced and kissed each other that made her wonder if they had gone to bed together.

She wasn't particularly shocked by the idea. Her own pattern of behavior was different but she had friends at home and at school, some of them girls younger than Janet, who had done the same thing. In fact, there were times when she wondered if any of her friends—she didn't exclude herself—would still be virgins when they got married.

What she objected to, where Janet and Rollie were concerned, was their using her as a smoke screen.

Her anger grew and hardened at the thought of it. She stood up and said, "We'd better get back. It must be almost dinner time."

They went into the house by the kitchen door. Mrs. Avery was busy at the sink. As she turned around it seemed to Mandy, from the sharp questioning glance she gave Janet and Rollie, that she must have some suspicion of their relationship. But all she said was, "Well, Janet, where have you been? I've been looking for you to set the table."

"Okay, no sweat," Janet said and moved leisurely into

the dining room. Rollie walked past her to the living room.

Mandy offered to help and made the salad. Just before dinner was ready to be served the phone rang. Janet answered it and called to Mrs. Avery, "It's for you, Mother."

She went to the phone. "Oh, Mrs. Lincoln," Mandy heard her say, "how nice of you to call. . . . No, I'm afraid she isn't. She's been losing a lot of ground lately. Dr. Cramer's not very hopeful—her age and all—but he's here every day doing what he can to keep her comfortable and free from pain. . . . Oh, I'm sorry, Mrs. Lincoln, but visitors are out of the question right now. She just isn't up to seeing anyone. But I'll tell her you called and I know she'll be pleased. Thank you very much. . . . Yes, I'll let you know. Good-by."

Mrs. Avery hung up and came back into the kitchen. "That was an old friend of my mother's," she said. "Wasn't it too bad I had to say she couldn't pay her a visit?"

At least there was still someone from the outside world who took an interest in the old lady's welfare, Mandy thought. But what good did it do when no one was allowed to see her?

It was still broad daylight outside when they sat down to dinner at six-thirty, but in the perpetual gloom of the dining room the overhead light had been turned on. Outside of its dim range dusk was pushing in from the corners of the room.

The meal was uninspired; fried chicken, not cooked quite enough, frozen peas, frozen french fries, sliced tomatoes and for dessert, ice cream, served with slightly stale cookies.

The older couple seemed preoccupied. The tension Mandy had noticed in them earlier in the day was more pronounced. Mrs. Avery directed a few animated remarks at her but was more often silent. Mr. Avery poked at the food on his plate but ate little of it and kept looking at his watch as if he had an appointment to keep. But if he had, he made no mention of it.

Rollie kept the conversation going. He talked about his exam that morning, the peculiarities of a hitchhiking soldier he had picked up on his way to Noroton and various experiences he'd had a few years ago when he had done some hitchhiking himself.

Most of what he said was addressed to Mandy, who was as tepid in response as she could allow herself to be without seeming as withdrawn as Janet, whose eyes were bright with anger whenever she looked at Rollie. She hardly spoke at all and seemed restless, too, getting to her feet ahead of Mrs. Avery to clear the table for dessert and bring in the coffee.

Before she sat down again the familiar cry of "Evelyn, I need you," came from upstairs, and without waiting to be told she went up to see what the old lady wanted.

She was back in two or three minutes. "Just a drink of water," she said.

A little after seven o'clock the meal was over. Mr. Avery, taking another look at his watch, pushed back his chair and said, "Well, I think I'll run into town. I've got a couple of errands to do. Need anything, Evelyn?"

"I guess not. Nothing for Mother, anyway. She's had her tray and I'll go up in a few minutes and get her settled for the night." Mrs. Avery spoke matter of factly but gave her husband an anxious look. "Take your time now and be sure you don't forget anything."

"Of course not." He was snappish but then, as he glanced at Mandy and Rollie, his tone changed. "Have a good time tonight, kids," he said benevolently treating them to his broadest smile.

"Yes, sure," Rollie said. "Maybe we should get going pretty soon, Mandy. The show must start fairly early this time of year and the drive-in's on the other side of town."

"Well, I'd better get going too," Mr. Avery said.

His wife's eyes followed him as he left the room. Whatever his errand, Mandy thought, it was a source of anxiety to her.

It wasn't to get anything for the old lady but probably had some connection with her. Everything seemed to revolve around her in one way or another; helpless and bedridden, she was still the dominant figure in the house.

Rollie got up from the table but Mandy remained seated, making up her mind to take charge of the situation. "Why don't you come with us tonight, Janet?" she said.

"Oh, I'll stay here." Janet's voice conveyed a note of martyrdom.

"Don't be silly. You might just as well come along with us."

Rollie, lighting a cigarette, didn't second the invitation. "Well—"

"No reason you shouldn't," Mandy urged.

"Oh, but there is," Mrs. Avery said. "I'd like her to keep an eye on Gran for a while and let me lie down in case I have to be up with her later tonight."

"I wouldn't think of going, anyway." Janet's glance went to Rollie. She added with the edge of malice that Mandy at last understood, "Three's always a crowd to you, isn't it, Regan?"

Regan? Mandy looked at him.

An ugly look came over his face. "Shut up," he said. "And cut out my middle name, too. You know how I feel about it."

"Too bad," Janet said, but her glance fell away from his.

"Finish clearing the table, Janet, and start the dishes. I've got to take care of Gran." Mrs. Avery stood up and went into the kitchen. A moment later they heard her going up the back stairs.

Janet began picking up the cups and saucers. "You'd better get ready for your date, Mandy," she said.

"Yes, let's get going." Rollie spoke abruptly, not looking at either of them.

"Well . . ." Mandy rose reluctantly and went upstairs to her room. She didn't want to go on this date—if that was what it should be called—and the incident at the table had deepened her reluctance.

She thought about it while she was brushing her hair and renewing her lipstick. There was some undercurrent, dark and complex, running through the relationship between Rollie and Janet, although she couldn't, for the life of her, imagine what it was.

It hadn't been the only undercurrent at dinner tonight, either. Something was bothering the Averys too. Maybe it had to do with their daughter's secret romance; more likely, she concluded moodily, taking a cardigan out of the bureau drawer and draping it around her shoulders, her earlier thought—that it had to do with Grandma Johnson—was more accurate. In this dreary old house all roads led to her.

Rollie was waiting in the living room. They went out through the kitchen. Janet, washing the dinner dishes, barely glanced at them over her shoulder. "Leaving?" she said. "Have fun."

"Oh, we will," Rollie said.

"'Bye for now," Mandy said.

They went out to his car. The cat, a safe distance away, watched their departure.

Mandy had seen the movie playing at the drive-in months before but didn't say so.

Rollie made a few efforts to flirt with her at first. She discouraged them by being brisk in her refusal to recognize them for what they were. After a while, his attentions became perfunctory, as if his thoughts were elsewhere.

On Janet, probably; the best way to get back into her good graces.

He had brought beer. During intermission he went to the refreshment stand for hamburgers and popcorn to eat with it. After he left the car Mandy went to the women's room and then walked over to the counter where he was just extricating himself from the crush with their order.

"Well, fancy meeting you here," he said, looking less than pleased at the sight of her.

She took the popcorn from him. "I thought you might need a helping hand, Regan," she said airily, using the name he disliked for some perverse reason she couldn't have explained if she had wanted to.

His reaction startled her. "You trying to be funny shouting that name around? I said I didn't like it, didn't I? Just forget it!"

"If that's the way you want it." There was frost in her voice. They walked back to the car in silence and in silence ate their hamburgers and drank the two cans of beer he opened. The silence would have lasted the rest of the night as far as Mandy was concerned. She'd had it, she told herself. She was fed up with Rollie, with Janet and her parents and the whole stupid visit.

Finally he said, "I'm sorry I blew my stack like that. I've got a thing, though, about my middle name."

"I'll say you have." Her voice went from frosty to neutral. It wasn't in her to nurse a grievance. She turned her head to look at him. "What have you got against it? I like it better than Rollie myself. It sort of stands out."

"It sure does, all right. Maybe that's why I don't like it." He smiled quizzically. "Maybe I'm a guy who doesn't want to stand out, who prefers to get lost in the crowd."

"Well, it's your name." She was bored with the subject and opened a bag of popcorn. Within the next few minutes the lights went off and the feature picture began.

It was one o'clock when they got back to the house.
Mandy said good night to Rollie and went upstairs ahead
of him. The doors were all closed. Everyone was in bed.

Rollie still hadn't come up when she was ready for bed.
Instead, she heard the door across the hall open quietly and
someone going downstairs. She opened her door a crack
and looked out just as Mr. Avery's head disappeared from
view on the stairs. A moment later the murmur of voices
came from the kitchen.

She shut her door and got into bed wondering what he
had to talk over with Rollie at one o'clock in the morning.
Perhaps it was nothing. The car driving in might have
awakened him and he might have gone downstairs for something to eat or a can of beer or anything at all.

But he hadn't got up right after their arrival. It almost
seemed as if he had waited, giving her time to undress, use
the bathroom and get back to her room before he made
his descent. In the meantime, Rollie hadn't come upstairs;
he had stayed downstairs in the kitchen as if he expected
the older man to join him.

Not that it meant anything to her whether they had got
together by design or by chance; whether they had arranged a private conference or were just talking over a can
of beer.

Nevertheless, although she couldn't have said why, she
found herself listening for them to come upstairs. Her eyes
picked out of the darkness the paler square of her open window with the shade drawn halfway. Night sounds reached
her, katydids in the fields heralding the end of summer,
wind rustling the leaves of the trees. Indoors there were
other sounds that she identified as the creakings of the old
house.

Her thoughts ranged far and wide. They touched on ad-
ditions she wanted to make to her shopping list for college;
her prospective roommate with whom she'd exchanged let-

ters this summer but who was still an unknown factor; the boy she'd met last month at Bar Harbor whom she had liked at first but who had turned out to be a complete fiasco; the visit Debbie, her roommate at boarding school, had promised to make over Labor Day; and finally, the family cottage, the gray shingled cottage on Penobscot Bay that seemed vastly remote in time and space, although it was only last Friday, three days ago, that she had left it and driven to her grandmother's in Bangor with her parents; it was only Saturday morning that she'd said good-by to them at the Bangor airport. She counted the hours—not yet seventy-two.

It seemed longer, like weeks, months, years ago. It seemed like forever.

Suddenly tears stung her eyes. Brushing them away, she admitted to herself that she was desperately homesick, more so than ever before in her life, even that first time she went to camp. She wanted her mother and father; she was sick for the sight of them.

Her tears came faster than she could brush them away. She turned her face into the pillow, until she had cried herself out. Then she slipped out of bed and, without reaching for the light, located her box of facial tissues and wiped her eyes and blew her nose.

She had forgotten about the two men downstairs, but her attention came back to them when she heard a car starting in the yard. She went to the side window and looked out. It was Rollie's car. He was using his parking lights as he backed it around and started down the driveway. He didn't turn on his brights until he reached the road and was headed toward Noroton.

It must be all of two o'clock, she thought. The only place he could be going as late as this was to an all-night restaurant. Perhaps he wanted something to eat that they didn't have in the house, like a pizza or a grinder. Or perhaps he had run out of cigarettes.

While she was still standing at the window the kitchen door was closed and the key turned in the lock. The light shining through the window went out. A moment later she heard Mr. Avery come upstairs. The door across the hall opened and closed.

Rollie, it seemed, wasn't expected back tonight.

It was one more peculiar little incident she could add to all the others that had taken place since her arrival Saturday.

She didn't feel like going back to bed just yet and sat down in the rocker by the window. There was a book of matches on the windowsill. She lit one and looked at her watch. Quarter past two. Tuesday morning, really, making it possible for her to say that it was the start of her last day in this house. Tomorrow was Wednesday, when she would be going to Bentonville. Sometime tomorrow night her parents were due back from their cruise. Thursday morning she would manage to call them from an outside phone and arrange for them to call her back at the Averys' with some excuse summoning her home right away. With luck, by Thursday afternoon—only about sixty hours or so from now —she would find herself at Hancock Airport boarding a plane for Boston.

It was comforting to think that tomorrow night her parents would no longer be out of reach but back at the cottage.

The house became still while she sat by the window, its creakings and settlings over with for the night. Only the sounds from outdoors broke the dead silence.

It got on Mandy's nerves. More wide awake than ever she tiptoed to her door, eased it open and looked out into the hall. It was pitch black except for a thin line of light shining under the door to the ell. Was the old lady shut up alone in there, or was Mrs. Avery sleeping in her room with her?

Apparently she was having a good night. No sound came from the ell, although Mandy stood listening for what seemed like a long time. At last she closed her door quietly and then froze against it as a wild mournful wail rose from outside her window. As it rose again, sad and terrible, like a lost child crying, she relaxed with a sigh of relief. It was only the cat, the poor homeless cat, crying its misery to the night.

She looked out the window. The wail rose again, but from farther away this time. Straining to see, she thought she could make out a dark shape drifting away across the lawn.

She glanced up at the sky. It was clouded over, with no stars visible. The wind had freshened and felt damp against her skin. It was probably going to rain tomorrow—today, rather—and that was all she needed, a rainy day cooped up in this dismal place.

She shivered suddenly and realized for the first time that she was cold. She went back to bed and pulled up the sheet and blanket over her.

Her thoughts settled on Rollie, his departure in the middle of the night and what reason he could have had for it. When speculation in that area proved fruitless, she found herself thinking about the way he had turned on her at the drive-in when she had called him by his middle name.

It was an unusual name. She would have expected him to prefer it to the more commonplace Rollie. Instead, he had got furious over it. Oh well—she yawned as sleep began to overtake her—why should she care when he meant nothing to her? None of them did. One thing was sure, though; after her own experience with a pen pal, she'd never let her children have one.

On that thought she fell asleep.

9

The first time Mandy woke up that morning it was a few minutes after eight. She looked at her watch and then looked out the window at the gray sky heavy with rain clouds. She closed her eyes and slipped back into a light sleep that was little more than dozing, waking up from it on and off until quarter of ten, when she finally got up to face the cheerless day.

She felt sluggish from her late night and thought wistfully of how helpful a shower would be as she went into the bathroom and ran water into the tub.

The bathroom seemed chilly and yet stickily humid; so did her bedroom when she got back to it. She debated closing the windows, but that would only shut in the dank smell that permeated the house. She dressed quickly, putting on an Oxford shirt and lightweight wool Bermudas and then felt more comfortable.

On her way downstairs she met Mrs. Avery, who came out of her room and said good morning with her artificially sweet smile.

"Sleep well, dear?" she said next.

"Yes, quite well. How is your mother this morning?"

"About the same. I hope the doctor didn't wake you. He was here a little while ago."

"Oh, was he? I didn't hear him. Did she have a good night?"

"After midnight, yes. She was pretty restless earlier but I gave her another sleeping pill at twelve o'clock and she slept right through until six. Well, I must get Janet up. That girl would sleep all day if I didn't wake her."

She knocked on Janet's door. "Janet, get up," she said.

"It's after ten o'clock. Mandy's up and dressed and I'm going down now to start her breakfast."

Mandy shook her head in annoyance, wishing that Mrs. Avery would get over the idea that she needed Janet's company every waking moment. But she couldn't very well tell her that as far as she was concerned, her daughter wouldn't be missed if she slept all day.

She went downstairs. The kitchen door stood open. She looked out. Mr. Avery's car was in the yard and he himself was wandering aimlessly about with his hands in his pockets. There was no sign of Rollie's car. Wherever he had gone, he hadn't got back yet.

The electric percolator was plugged in and two places were set at the kitchen table. The girl poured juice for herself and took eggs out of the refrigerator, prepared to get her own breakfast.

She heard the old lady calling to Mrs. Avery. Listening to the high cracked voice, Mandy pictured her as a scrawny little woman with a hunched figure, nutcracker jaw and chin and wispy white hair. She smiled at the thought, realizing that what she was conjuring up was a witch from the fairy tales of her childhood.

While she was frying eggs for herself Mrs. Avery descended the back stairs and deplored the fact that Mandy had been left to get her own breakfast. She made the toast and poured a cup of coffee for herself when the girl said that she preferred milk.

They sat down opposite each other at the table. The gray morning light from a nearby window did Mrs. Avery no favors. It showed up the pitted, grainy texture of her skin, found brassy highlights in her dyed hair and a smear of lipstick at the corner of her mouth. It was a coarse mouth, Mandy thought. Her whole face was coarse, the forehead too low, the jaw outthrust, almost a lantern jaw. She looked rather like a prison matron.

It was surprising, the girl thought next, that her mother had liked Mrs. Avery so much that she had encouraged Mandy's pen pal friendship with Janet. But perhaps Mrs. Avery's basic coarseness had been less obvious nine or ten years ago. Or her mother might not have noticed it in their few days' acquaintance.

"Well, well," Janet said from the hall doorway, "breakfast is being served, I see." She advanced across the kitchen and sat down with them. "I guess I'll just have juice and coffee," she said. "I'm dead. I hate getting up in the morning. Where's Rollie? I figured if I had to get up he should get up too, but when I went in his room he wasn't there."

"He's been up since eight o'clock. He went in town." Mrs. Avery added reprovingly, "You shouldn't be running in and out of his room, Janet. After all, even if he is your cousin, it doesn't look right."

"Oh, for God's sake."

"Now, Janet—"

"Forget it. Pour my coffee, will you?"

Mrs. Avery reddened with anger but made no reply. She poured the coffee.

Janet reached for her cigarettes and lighted one. "Left mine upstairs," she said.

Mandy made up speeches in her head while she finished her breakfast. Such as: "Will you kindly explain to me, Mrs. Avery, why you just told that whopper about Rollie; not that I give a damn where he is but I do wonder why you felt you had to lie about it." Or, simple and direct, "What the hell is going on around here, Mrs. Avery? Are you and your whole family nuts?" Or, best of all, "Drive me to the bus station right away, Mrs. Avery. I want to get out of here as fast as I can."

It was too bad that none of her speeches could be delivered.

Her next thought was that she seemed to spend most of

her time brooding about something or other connected with the Averys. It was fantastic that she should bother, considering how brief her visit was to be and her intention never to have anything to do with them again once it was over.

She couldn't help it, though, no matter how fantastic it was. Maybe it wasn't fantastic at all, considering that the odd little things, like the lie just now about Rollie, kept piling up, none of them too big in itself but cumulative in effect to the point where her feeling that there was something queer, something wrong going on in this house, kept growing stronger. It colored her attitude toward every member of the family. Even the poor old lady upstairs, around whom most of her worries were centered, she had pictured as looking like a witch.

She wouldn't try to tell herself again to get off this treadmill. She was on it to stay.

She got up from the table. "I'll do the dishes while you're getting dressed, Janet," she said.

Mrs. Avery protested, was patiently overridden, and then said that she had to give her mother a bed bath. She went upstairs with Janet and Mandy had the kitchen to herself.

While she was clearing the table Rollie drove into the yard but didn't come into the house. Mr. Avery, who was still outside, went hurrying over to the car as if he had been waiting for Rollie to arrive. They disappeared in back of the house, but a moment later from the kitchen window Mandy saw them go into the grape arbor and sit down on the bench, deep in conversation. Rollie was wearing the chino pants he'd had on last night at the drive-in, but a different shirt. He must have gone to Syracuse, she thought. Most of his clothes would be in his room there.

When the dishes were done she stood irresolute in the middle of the kitchen. Overhead, footsteps moved to and fro and water ran in the lavatory. Then she heard Mrs.

Avery call, "Come and help me with Gran's bed, Janet," and some sort of reply from the front of the house.

She looked out the window again. The conference—a continuation of last night's, perhaps?—was still going on in the arbor. Rollie wasn't playing the admiring beau today, she reflected sardonically. He hadn't come rushing in to greet her.

She wandered into the living room, drearier than ever on this gray day. She didn't know what to do with herself. Then her glance fell on the oak desk in the corner. She might as well write to Debbie and tell her how awful this whole thing was. Begin it Dear Cassandra because just last week Debbie had written her that a visit to a pen pal was bound to turn out a ghastly flop.

Mandy opened the desk front. Empty cubbyholes confronted her. The small center drawer held the stub of a pencil, nothing else. Funny. Her dark winged brows drew together in a frown. She closed the desk front and then, ignoring a guilty sense of prying, opened the drawers of the lower section. A spool of thread in one, a bookmark in another. That was all.

Still frowning, she walked away from the desk and came to a halt in the dining room doorway. She looked into the room, hesitated for a moment and then went over to the sideboard. The drawers, lined with yellowed paper, had next to nothing in them; the plastic tablecloth Mrs. Avery used for meals, a few dustcloths and odds and ends.

She went back into the living room and sat down, reaching for a magazine so that she would at least look occupied if anyone came into the room.

But until that happened, she was free to let her gaze settle on the empty desk. It had been cleaned out. Not recently, though. The cubbyholes had a thick coat of dust.

Mrs. Avery, it seemed, hadn't been able to wait until her mother was dead to go through her papers. Vulturelike, she had cleaned out the desk on some earlier visit. But why take everything when most of it couldn't have had any particular value?

The nurse was probably the answer. There'd been one in the house for months and she would have been an obstacle to a leisurely sorting out process. Mrs. Avery, to keep her mother from finding out what she was doing, had just dumped everything in the desk into a carton or suitcase and taken it home to look through it.

It made a nasty little picture. Even nastier, in a way, were the empty drawers in the dining room. Undoubtedly Mrs. Avery had searched them and every other drawer in the house for the money but she hadn't been looking for a clue to its whereabouts when she helped herself to her mother's linens and silver.

She had known her mother would never get downstairs again to find out what she had done. It was a ghoulish robbing of the almost dead. A pointless robbing, too, when all she had to do was wait a little while and she would inherit everything her mother had.

But was she the only heir? Perhaps this was something Mandy shouldn't take for granted. The old lady might have blood relatives, nieces or nephews, who were to share her estate with Mrs. Avery, her adopted daughter.

But if that were the reason for stealing from her, wouldn't the other heirs demand an accounting when the old lady died?

Mandy sat puzzling over it, having only the vaguest knowledge of the laws of inheritance. Then her expression cleared as she remembered what Janet had said about her grandmother, in her senility, selling things out of the house last year. Mandy had thought it was just furniture she had sold, as in the closed-off parlor, but apparently it had been much more than that. Linens, silver and—her glance surveyed the room—bric-a-brac, pictures and ornaments had also been sold. She hadn't paid enough attention to it until now, but the lack of these small touches was one of the main reasons for the bleak look of the house. It was not only dilapidated; it had been stripped down to the barest essentials.

The old lady must be in a terribly confused state to have sold most of her belongings out of purely imaginary poverty. She had given the Averys ample justification to consider her a burden. And if they had found her money since the desk was emptied out they had no need to prolong her life.

But needing to prolong it and deliberately shortening it were two things poles apart.

Well, here she was back on that, Mandy reflected. Sunday night's tray and the old lady's cry that she was hungry had taken root in her mind.

All right, go over that familiar ground again. There'd been a nurse in the house until Saturday and a new one was due tonight. Mrs. Avery couldn't possibly starve the old lady to death when she was only taking care of her for three days. There was the doctor too. He came every day and his suspicions would soon be aroused if the old lady kept complaining that she was hungry.

Did he come every day though? Mandy put down the magazine. She had yet to lay eyes on him herself. Sunday morning Mrs. Avery had said he had come while she and Janet were at church and yesterday while they were doing the grocery shopping in Noroton.

This morning, according to Mrs. Avery, he had paid his visit much earlier while Mandy was still in bed. But how early? She had first waked up at eight o'clock and had only dozed after that. Looking back on it now, it seemed strange that she hadn't heard the doctor at all.

This was the wildest idea she'd had yet, she told herself. Mrs. Avery couldn't be withholding medical attention from the old lady. Just last night on the phone she'd told a friend of her mother's that the doctor came every day. She wouldn't have dared lie about it. In a small city like Noroton there was a perfectly good chance that the woman herself or some friend of hers went to the same doctor and might happen to mention his daily visits to Mrs. Avery's mother.

But it still seemed strange that she hadn't heard him at all this morning.

The kitchen door opened and someone came in. Mandy reached for the magazine and began to turn the pages. The next moment Rollie entered the room.

"Well, good morning," he said. "I didn't think you were ever going to get up."

"Oh, I've been up quite a while." She gave him a guileless look. "I saw you and Mr. Avery in the grape arbor but you seemed to be having such a serious talk that I didn't want to break in on it. Settling world problems, it looked like."

"That's right." He sat down on the sofa. "Who's going to hit the most home runs in the American League this year."

He gave her a grin. He hadn't even bothered to make up a convincing lie, she thought. He was letting her know that the conversation outside was none of her business. Which it wasn't, of course.

The phone rang. Another old friend of Grandma Johnson's inquiring about her? If Mandy had been alone she would have been tempted to pick it up just for the reassurance she would get from hearing someone else inquiring about the old lady and being told that the doctor came every day. Even hearing the phone ring—it didn't ring often—was reassuring as a reminder that she wasn't completely isolated from the outside world. She needed such reminders. She was reduced to it by this house. She'd be listening at doors next if she didn't watch out.

On the second ring the phone was answered upstairs. It wasn't necessarily someone calling about the old lady.

"How long since Grandma Johnson's been able to have visitors?" she asked Rollie.

"Couldn't tell you," he replied. "She's been pretty bad all summer, I guess. I've only met her once myself. They took me in and introduced me the first time I came here back in June. Even then she was quite feeble and didn't seem to know which end was up. Art says she's gone completely batty now but occasionally has lucid moments." Rollie paused before he added, "What made you ask?"

The girl shrugged. "Just wondered."

"Nothing better to do around here, is there? Well, that's the story. It must be an awful nuisance, though, taking care of her."

"But she's dying, isn't she?"

"Looks that way. Cigarette?"

"Yes, I'll have one."

When he had given her one and lighted one for himself he stood looking out the window for a moment before he sat down again. "Hell of a gloomy day," he said. "I thought we'd go for a swim this afternoon, but it's going to rain. We'll have to find something else to do."

"If Janet's free," Mandy said pointedly.

He raised his eyebrows at this, but before he could make any comment Janet came running downstairs. "That was Dick who just called, Mandy," she announced as she rushed into the room. "He was going to drive all the way up here tonight with Mark Benham—I've told you about Mark, haven't I?—but when I explained that Mother and Dad were going to Bentonville tonight to pick up the nurse and that I'd have to take care of Gran, he said he'd fix you up for tomorrow night after we get home. He's making all kinds of plans for the rest of the week, too. Give me a cigarette, will you, Rollie?"

He gave her a cigarette and lighted it. She dropped into a chair and blew smoke rings at the ceiling as she continued, "Dick asked me what we were doing for excitement out here in the sticks and I told him we managed to keep busy. He sounded so jealous!"

Mandy stole a glance at Rollie. He showed no sign of the jealousy Janet ascribed to Dick. Yesterday they had been in each other's arms, but now they were acting as if they meant nothing to each other.

It was beyond her, one more thing that she couldn't figure out.

10

Mandy went up to her room be-
fore lunch and got out the postcard she had bought for her
grandmother. She wrote on the message side, "Hi, Gran.
We've been here in Noroton with Janet's grandmother ever
since I arrived Saturday. Tomorrow we're leaving for Bentonville. See you soon. Lots of love, Mandy."

She started to put it in her pocketbook after she had addressed it but changed her mind and left it in plain sight
on the bureau so that she wouldn't forget to mail it.

No one had a stamp when she asked about it at lunch.

"Is it a postcard you want to mail?" Mrs. Avery inquired.

"Yes, it's to my grandmother."

"Well, I'd be glad to mail it for you. We go right by the
Noroton post office on our way to Bentonville."

"Oh, thank you. I'll give it to you before you go."

"Don't you think you'd better run up and get it now so
you won't forget? My pocketbook's out in the kitchen and
I'll put it with a letter I have to mail." Mrs. Avery added
with a smile, "I just want to make sure your grandmother
hears from you."

Her insistence seemed uncalled for to Mandy—after all,
she had purposely left the card out on the bureau—but she
went upstairs and came down with it.

As the older woman took it from her she said, "Aren't you
going to send one to your parents?"

"I thought I'd call them from Bentonville."

"Oh, I see."

Lunch was the same as yesterday, sandwiches made from
cold cuts and a salad of sliced tomatoes and cucumbers.

Mandy helped Janet with the dishes. Mrs. Avery put a dish of canned applesauce, toast and a glass of milk on a tray and took it upstairs.

Mandy looked out the window while she was drying the dishes. A drizzle of rain had begun to fall. She would go right through the roof, she thought, if she didn't get out of here pretty soon.

Rollie rescued her. He came in from outdoors with Mr. Avery and said, "How about going to Fulton with me this afternoon, Mandy? I told a friend of mine there that I might look him up some day this week."

"Sure, why not?" She kept her tone casual, not wanting to reveal how eager she was to get away from the house. She dried the last dish, spread the towel out on the rack and turned to Janet. "How about it, Janet?"

Before Janet could reply Mr. Avery intervened. "I think, Mandy, that you and Rollie had better go without her," he said. "Her mother and I are planning to start for Bentonville around five-thirty—I've got a couple of things to see to at the store before we pick up the nurse—and if anything held you kids up, we couldn't very well go off and leave Janet's grandmother alone."

Janet eyed him rebelliously. "But what if Rollie plans to get back before five-thirty?" she said.

"No. When you go somewhere in a car there's no guarantee that you'll be back right on time."

"My God," she muttered, "what do you think I'm made of? I'll have the screaming meemies if I'm stuck in this morgue much longer."

"Janet!" His voice was like the crack of a whip. "Didn't we make it plain before we came here that we expected full co-operation from you? You know it's the last day and you'd just better make up your mind to do as you're told."

Mandy shot a glance at him and looked away quickly astonished by the ugly threatening look on his face that went, she thought, far beyond what the situation called for. He was in a real sweat about something, more so than yesterday. She'd be afraid of him herself in his present mood.

Janet was cowed by it. "Okay," she said sullenly. "You don't have to make a production out of it. I'll stay."

Rollie, lounging in a chair, watched the two alertly but in silence.

"I'll just get my raincoat," Mandy said to him and made her escape upstairs. She had no intention of playing the amiable guest offering to stay home with Janet. She would have the screaming meemies herself if she had to sit around the house all afternoon. Today was the worst day of all.

As she got her raincoat out of her closet, she glanced around her comfortless room. It was surprising how much difference sunshine had made the past two days. Just to look out the windows at it had helped. Going to church in Noroton, doing the shopping there, spending both afternoons at the pond and then getting away last night had helped. Looking back on it, she had to concede that under the circumstances, the Averys were doing what they could to keep her occupied with a minimum amount of her time spent in the house.

She threw her raincoat over her arm and went out into the hall, closing her door after her.

All the other doors were closed. The only light came from a small stained-glass window set high in the wall at the head of the stairs. As she started down them she was suddenly assailed by the feeling of being very much alone in alien surroundings. She stopped short for a moment, her foot suspended between one tread and the next. Her feeling of aloneness, of What - am - I - doing - here - in - this - house-among-these-people? was followed by a feeling even more frightening: that the house was worse than alien, that there was some sort of evil in it.

How silly could she get? She set her foot down firmly on

the next tread. A house was an inanimate object. It couldn't be anything, one way or another. Of course not.

Unless—she stopped short again, her flesh prickling—it could somehow absorb evil from evil occupants.

This wasn't just silly; it was practically hysterical. And what was its basis? A few odd little happenings, attitudes, displays of tension, an atmosphere she was building up herself because of the way she felt toward the people in the house. It all stemmed from that, from her intense dislike of them.

No, not all of it. Fear—the thought caught her unawares—came into it.

Fear? They had done nothing to give rise to it. Why should it touch her?

She didn't know. She only knew that whatever its cause she felt it.

"Mandy, what's keeping you?" Rollie came out into the hall.

"Coming," she said and ran down the rest of the stairs.

The drizzle had stopped when they got outside, but the sky was dark with the promise of rain. As they got into the car they heard a distant clap of thunder presaging what was to come.

"We're going to get a hell of a big storm before the day is over," Rollie said.

He turned right on the road, following the same route Mandy had traveled with Janet. She glanced at the first farm they passed. It was no closer to the old lady's house than the nearest neighbor going in the other direction toward Noroton. She commented on it to Rollie and added, "I can't imagine how she's stood being all alone in that house since her husband died."

"She was used to it, I guess."

"Did she ever have a car so that she could get away if she wanted to?"

"I don't think so."

"I'd die if I had to stay there."

"Well, you don't." His tone dismissed the subject.

Mandy's moment of fright on the stairs had passed as soon as she was out of the house, but it left her with a feeling of disquiet. She became aware of it when they reached a main highway and she found herself looking at roadside establishments, a boy mowing a lawn, children playing in a yard, as if these were things she had never seen before or was coming back to after a long absence.

The feeling persisted when they arrived in Fulton. She took pleasure in the sight of people on the street and the sense of life around her. She hoped she would like Rollie's friend and that he lived in a bright cheerful house.

But she wasn't to meet him. Rollie stopped at a drugstore and said he'd better go in and phone him before they started hunting him up. He was shaking his head when he came out and got back into the car.

"Doug isn't home," he said. "His mother's not expecting him until evening."

"Well, we had a nice drive, anyway," Mandy said.

He nodded. "Better than sitting around the house."

"Maybe we should walk around a bit before we start back," she suggested, wanting to delay their return.

"Let's get out of town first. Then we'll stop somewhere and have a beer."

He pulled up at a tavern on Route 11 that was as dark and cheerless as the house they were returning to. The lackadaisical bartender served them and went back to his conversation with a man at the bar.

Mandy looked at her watch. It was ten after three. "We should be back before the Averys leave," she said. "Janet could have come with us, after all."

"I suppose so. I could see Art's point, though."

As always, his tone was neutral in speaking of Janet. But

today it wasn't because he was playing up to Mandy. He made conversation, treated her to one of his best smiles every now and then, but showed a tendency to lapse into his own thoughts, not particularly pleasant, to judge from the hard look that came to his face.

Mandy wondered if his thoughts were connected with the Averys or the old lady. Not that the old lady concerned him; she wasn't related to him in any way; he had seen her only once early in the summer and had nothing to gain by her death.

He had seen her, though. . . .

"What does Mrs. Johnson look like?" she asked.

"Look like? What brought that up?"

"Oh, I've just been thinking about her, the way you do about people. Her voice makes me picture her as a scrawny little woman with a sharp nose and chin and wispy white hair."

He laughed. "Like a witch?"

"That's exactly what I thought of. What is she really like?"

"Well, let's see. . . . I didn't study her looks, but I don't recall her being scrawny. In fact, rather plump, I'd say."

Plump in June didn't necessarily mean plump in August.

"A perfectly ordinary-looking old lady," Rollie continued. "White hair is the only thing you were right about."

"Short or long?" Mandy was trying to form a reasonably accurate picture of Mrs. Avery's mother.

"I don't remember. Yes, I do. She had braids tied with pink ribbons."

"She sounds like rather a sweet-looking old lady."

"I guess she is."

Pink ribbons didn't fit in with Mandy's concept of the kind of treatment the old lady was receiving. But then, there'd been a nurse in charge when Rollie had met her and she would keep her patient fixed up.

It would be interesting to know if there'd been pink ribbons since the nurse left.

Rollie retreated into his own thoughts again.

She looked at him. She doubted that it would bother him much if he suspected that the Averys were doing anything to hasten the old lady's death. That was the kind of an impression he had made on her in their brief acquaintance.

He finished his beer and said, "There's no reason we have to stick around the house tonight just because Janet does. Let's go out to dinner. There's a restaurant north of Watertown on the St. Lawrence River where they serve wonderful seafood. Like to try it?"

"Yes, but we'd be gone quite a while, wouldn't we?"

"All the better. It's not that far, anyway. Maybe thirty-five, forty miles."

"Okay." She spoke hesitantly and then added, "Janet's not going to like it, though, being left alone all evening with her grandmother."

"Her tough luck," he said.

Janet, Mandy thought, had picked herself a real beaut in Rollie.

The sky had not lightened but the storm held off, no closer, it seemed, when they got back to the house than when they had left it. Mr. Avery's car was still in the yard. Janet could have gone with them and had a few hours of freedom before she was left alone with the old lady.

Mandy would have felt guiltier about leaving her or would have insisted on staying home to keep her company if they had been on more congenial terms. But as it was, her thoughts ran in self-justification, they had nothing to say to each other. Janet didn't act as if she particularly wanted her around. Mandy, therefore, should have no qualms about getting out of the house whenever she could.

Not that she looked forward to going out with Rollie. Back home she wouldn't have accepted his invitation to dinner.

But when it was a choice between him and the house, he was much the lesser of two evils.

The cat was in the yard when they got out of the car.

"There's that lousy cat again." He took a menacing step toward it.

The cat ran away.

"I'll kill it yet," he said.

Mandy was silent. They went into the house.

11

The Averys were nearly ready to leave, Mr. Avery waiting for his wife in the kitchen. Janet came yawning out of the living room. She'd taken a nap, she said. Nothing else to do.

"Well, you didn't miss anything, not coming with us," Rollie informed her. "I called Doug and he wasn't home so we turned right around and came back."

"Didn't you stop at all?" Mr. Avery asked.

"Just for a beer."

"How exciting." Janet widened her china doll eyes derisively at Rollie.

He gave her a cold glance but before he could reply Mrs. Avery came down the back stairs, her raincoat over her arm.

"Oh, so you're back," she greeted them. "Horrible day, isn't it? It's got so sticky I wish it would hurry up and rain and get it over with. I have your postcard right here, Mandy." She patted her pocketbook. "I won't forget to mail it in Noroton."

"Thank you," the girl said.

Mrs. Avery turned to Janet. "There are cube steaks and frozen green beans for dinner, dear. Put some potatoes in to bake."

"Mandy and I won't be here," Rollie announced. "We're going out to dinner."

"Well, that's just fine." Mr. Avery beamed at them. "I'm glad you're going to entertain Mandy for us, Rollie. Too bad Janet has to stay here, but it can't be helped."

"It's just one of those things." Janet glared openly at Rollie.

"Yes, it is." He looked back at her imperturbably. "Otherwise, we'd ask you to come along."

"This is the last time you'll have to take care of Gran, dear." Mrs. Avery's tone was placating. "The last time. Isn't it going to be wonderful to have a nurse here to take over her care?"

"Just wonderful," Janet said. "Just divine. Dear, dear grandmother."

"Now, Janet." Arthur Avery frowned at her. "Don't speak to your mother that way." He took his wife's arm. "Let's get going."

"Oh, Gran's supper," she said. "There's a can of chicken soup in the cupboard, Janet. Give her that. It's the last can in the house, though, so you'd better remind me to get some more in the morning. I'll make out a store order before we leave. Then there's a dish of pudding in the refrigerator. With tea and toast that will be all she'll want. She's asleep now but she'll be ready for her supper when she wakes up. And fix yourself a cube steak."

"Yes, Mother," Janet drawled, on the edge of insolence.

Mrs. Avery ignored her tone. She smiled at Mandy and said, "Have a nice evening now."

"What time are you picking up the nurse?" Rollie asked.

"Oh, a little after eight. We'll be back by eleven."

Mr. Avery tugged at her arm. "Come on, Evelyn, or we won't even get there tonight."

"All right," she said.

They went out the kitchen door to the car.

"Well, they're gone," Rollie said as the car started up. "They're on their way."

"Yes," said Janet. "On their way."

They were declaring a truce, it seemed. Some hidden meaning lay beneath their words and exchange of glances. But they had no privacy they could take advantage of now that the Averys were gone. She herself was still there, the fifth wheel.

"I'll make us a drink," Rollie said.

"I'd just as soon have a beer," Mandy said.

"Okay." He took a can of beer out of the refrigerator. "You're in luck, kid. I didn't think there was any left."

He opened the can for her and mixed rye and water for Janet and himself.

They sat down at the table. As Mandy picked up the can Janet said, "Lot of calories in that. Better watch out."

"I'll worry about it later."

"Like ten years later?" Janet giggled as if she had said something remarkably funny, and kept it up until Rollie said in a sharp voice, "That's enough. Cut it out, Janet."

Mandy drank her beer and looked at her. That idiotic giggle, almost out of control, pointed to another little mystery going on around here. It didn't matter. She was sick and tired of everything that had to do with the Averys and was just waiting for Thursday to see the last of them.

Maybe she wouldn't wait that long. Maybe tomorrow, on the way to Bentonville, she'd tell them she wanted to go home and ask to be dropped off at the Syracuse airport. Let their feelings be hurt. She was past caring about that; and besides, how much attention did they pay to hers? Her pen pal Janet paid none. She had turned out to be an utter fink.

Mandy finished her beer and got to her feet. "Guess I'll go up and change now," she said.

"Lucky you, going out to dinner," Janet said. "Make me another drink, Rollie." She leaned back to reach the radio on the counter behind her and turned it full blast on a rock 'n' roll station.

"For God's sake, you trying to wake up your grandmother?" Rollie exclaimed. "Turn it down."

"Oh well. . . ." She went off into another giggling fit, but she turned down the radio.

Her giggle sounded even more out of control; she could as easily have been crying as laughing, Mandy thought on the way upstairs. She'd probably had a big scene with her parents over having to take care of her grandmother to-night.

The door to the ell was closed, but soon after Mandy went into her own room she heard the shrill cracked voice calling for Janet and then heard her come upstairs. Turning the radio on loud had backfired on her.

Mandy got washed and dressed quickly, wanting to get out of the house. Rollie seemed to feel the same way. He came upstairs and took possession of the bathroom as soon as she vacated it.

When she was dressed she stood at the bureau touching her wrists and throat and earlobes with French perfume her grandmother had given her on her birthday. Then she stepped back to look at herself in the mirror, reflecting that at least she was getting a chance to wear the only dress-up outfit she had brought with her.

Her dress was a sleeveless navy-blue silk sheath worn with matching pumps, short white gloves and white earrings.

She took another look at herself as she picked up her navy-blue clutch bag. Sometimes her French twist didn't come out right, no matter how much she fussed with it, but to-night she could find no fault with it. She had achieved the smooth elegant effect that was just what she wanted. Too much eye shadow? No, not for evening. It was flattering to her eyes; it brought out their deep blue color.

She went on looking at herself a moment longer. The mirror gave back her slim young figure, delicate features and clean-skinned, glowing look, the look of a girl who had been cherished and cared for from the day of her birth.

She went out into the hall. She heard Rollie moving around in his room and voices from the wing indicating that Janet was still with her grandmother.

She went downstairs. The front hall was so dark that she turned on the light. It was only six o'clock, but the storm that had held off all day was bringing in an early twilight. She'd better take along her raincoat, she thought.

It was in the kitchen where she had left it. Her beer can and Rollie's glass still stood on the table, but Janet's glass was missing. She must have taken her drink upstairs with her.

She should be coming down any minute, though, to get her grandmother's supper. She couldn't have given it to her yet; there were no signs of its preparation.

The old lady would be lucky if she got any supper at all with Janet in charge of it.

But even as Mandy was thinking this she heard footsteps overhead and a moment later Janet came downstairs and out into the kitchen with Rollie in her wake.

Her glance swept over Mandy. "Good-looking outfit," she said.

Rollie whistled. "It sure is."

Mandy laughed. "All right, let's just admit that we both look pretty sharp tonight."

He was wearing a Glen plaid jacket, dark slacks, gray shirt and narrow black tie. He looked immaculate. "Thanks for the kind words," he said. "Let's be on our way."

"Have a real blast," Janet said.

"Sorry you can't come along," Mandy told her.

Janet shrugged. "Oh, I'll live through it."

They went out to Rollie's car. He started the motor and then frowned as his glance fell on the barn door.

"Art forgot to lock the door," he said.

The padlock hung loose from the handle. Rollie got out of the car, went over to the barn and snapped it shut.

"What does Mr. Avery keep in there that he's so careful of?" Mandy asked when he came back to the car.

"Some expensive tools he wouldn't want stolen. He's been fixing the floor or something."

"I can't imagine anyone coming way out here to steal," she said.

"You never know. That was pretty careless of Art."

Mr. Avery had been more preoccupied than careless, she thought, with whatever he'd had on his mind all day, he and the rest of them.

She looked at the barn as Rollie backed the car around. Fixing the floor seemed a waste of time when the whole structure was ready to fall apart.

A pale sun showed itself briefly just north of Watertown but was soon obliterated by a black mass of clouds banked across the horizon. Dusk settled swiftly after that. At seven-thirty they reached the restaurant on the St. Lawrence.

Rollie had two martinis before dinner, Mandy an Alexander. They ordered broiled lobster. It was delicious Mandy said, adding with a smile, "Almost as good as the ones we have in Maine."

He played up to her. "And they're the world's best?"

"Of course. Any Mainer, even a part-time one, knows that."

He appeared to listen as she went on talking about Maine but left most of the conversation to her, his mood as remote as it had been that afternoon. But it was more tense now, she thought. His dark brooding face had tension written all over it. She asked him finally what was the matter.

"Nothing," he replied. "Why should there be?"

"I just wondered," she said.

He came alive then for a little while, announcing that he had his own plans made for her when they got to Bentonville tomorrow; he wasn't going to let Janet tie her up with double dates the rest of the week. He didn't care much for Janet's friends, anyway; they'd have more fun by themselves.

It was all shallow patter off the top of his head. He didn't

mean a word of it, she thought, and gave him so little en-
couragement that he soon lapsed into himself.

By nine o'clock they had finished their dinner and were
leaving the restaurant. The wind had risen while they were
inside. Thunder rumbled in the distance like a threatening
beast of the jungle.

Once they were clear of the parking lot Rollie pushed his
little Renault up to sixty and then to sixty-five. They would
beat the storm home, he said, sounding gay, almost wild as
if the wind were sweeping away his tensions and injecting
him with new vigor and confidence. In a strong baritone he
roared out, "Blow the man down, blow the man down, blow,
blow, blow the man down . . ."

"Barnacle Bill the Sailor" came next. He broke off in the
middle of it and said, "Storms get into my blood, kid. They
make me wild as a hawk. When it's my time to die I want
to go out in one. The bigger the better. How about you,
baby? How do you feel?"

"We'll both go out in a storm right now if you don't cut
out the old salt bit," Mandy said apprehensively as the little
car, pushed up to seventy, rocked and swerved in the wind.
"Take it easy, will you?"

"What's the matter, you want to stick around this great
big wonderful world?" His tone mocked her, but he eased
his foot off the accelerator and brought the car down to
sixty.

It didn't take them much more than an hour to get home.
A little after ten the house, lighted upstairs and down, rose
out of the dark ahead of them and for once Mandy was
glad to see it in her relief that the ride was over. There had
been other flourishes and reckless bursts of speed from
Rollie along the way; he turned off the road almost on two
wheels, singing at the top of his lungs that he was a honky-
tonk man from a honky-tonk town and slamming the car to
a stop at the kitchen door.

"It was a lovely ride," she said to him sweetly as she got out of the car. "I enjoyed every minute of it."

"So did I." He laughed and squeezed her arm. "Now I'll make us a tall cold drink. Janet will certainly need one. I'll bet she feels sorry for herself, stuck here with her grandmother all night."

The first flash of lightning streaked across the sky as they went into the house.

"You see, baby?" Rollie said, holding the door for her. "If I hadn't driven like hell I wouldn't have got you home nice and dry. Sir Walter Raleigh without a cloak, that's me."

"Forget it." Mandy's tone closed the subject.

The kitchen seemed bright as she went into it out of the rising storm. It seemed almost to welcome her on this, her last night in the house.

12

Janet had a Duke Ellington record on in the living room. She turned off the record player and came out to the kitchen, her hair up on rollers.

"Gee, I'm glad you got back before the storm breaks," she greeted them. "I was getting the jitters alone here with no one but Gran. Much company she'd be. I gave her a sleeping pill after she'd had her supper and she's been sleeping like the dead ever since."

"Well, at least you got your hair done," Mandy said.

"I did my nails over too." Janet raised her hands for inspection. "Had to kill time somehow." She felt her hair. "It's dry," she said. "How about making us a drink, Rollie, while I go take the rollers out? I'd better look in on Gran, too."

She went up the back stairs, closing the door after her.

"Well, let's see about that drink." Rollie opened the cupboard and took out a jigger and three glasses. "Get out some ice cubes, will you?" he said to Mandy. "And club soda for you."

She got a tray of ice cubes and a bottle of club soda out of the refrigerator, pushed the door shut with her elbow and then realized belatedly that the dish of pudding Janet was supposed to have given her grandmother stood untouched on one of the shelves.

She brought the ice cubes and soda over to Rollie, who had set the glasses and liquor on the drainboard. There were dirty dishes in the sink. She looked at them. A frying pan—the cube steak—a cake tin with a French fried potato stuck to it, a small saucepan—to boil water for instant coffee from the jar left out on the drainboard—one cup and saucer, one plate, one fork, knife and spoon and a spatula. There were no dishes from the old lady's supper. Janet hadn't fed her at all.

Rollie noticed the dirty dishes when he ran water over the ice cubes to loosen them. His scowl made it plain that he hadn't missed their significance, but he kept his tone light as he remarked, "Well, I see Janet's left the dishes. Pretty slack, that gal."

The phone rang just then. "I'd better get it." He headed quickly for the dining room. "It's probably Art or Evelyn."

At the same moment Mandy heard Janet run into the ell to pick up the phone there.

This was Mandy's chance to verify what she already knew.

The can of chicken soup was in the first cupboard she opened. She read the label, CHICKEN SOUP WITH RICE, as if she might be making a mistake, but there it was, bringing into sharp focus all her doubts and fears about the kind of care the old lady was getting.

She closed the cupboard door and sat down at the table. No supper at all, she thought. Not even tea and toast, or there would have been another cup and saucer and plate added to the dishes in the sink.

Was Janet just too lazy to bother feeding her grand-mother? That couldn't be the answer when she had left the food where her mother would see it.

It had been deliberate on Janet's part. There must be, as Mandy had felt all along, a plot to starve the old lady to death. Not by flagrant starvation that the doctor would no-tice, but by weakening her a little more each day.

That didn't take into account, though, the nurse who was arriving—or was due to arrive—tonight. There was nothing to keep the Averys from saying that at the last minute she couldn't come. Or, if they brought her back with them, from letting her go as soon as Mandy's visit was over.

But in the latter case, why let Mandy come at all when they could have pleaded the old lady's illness?

Perhaps they were thinking of questions being raised later on and wanted Mandy there as a witness to the good care the old lady was receiving.

What was she going to do if they came back without the nurse? She couldn't just take a plane home tomorrow and forget about it. She had to do something, she didn't know what.

Lost in conjecture, she had been only vaguely aware of Rollie's voice on the phone, but at this point she heard him say good-by and hang up.

"That was Art," he informed her, coming back to the kitchen. "They're on their way. They'll be here in another hour."

"Are they bringing the nurse?"

"Oh yes, she's with them."

At least she was coming; the weight of an immediate decision was lifted.

Rollie caught the look of relief on Mandy's face and grinned. "What's the matter, were you afraid you'd be stuck out here after tomorrow?"

"Just asking." She got to her feet, picked up her raincoat and put her clutch bag in the pocket.

"Where are you going?" he inquired.

"Out on the porch to see how the storm's coming. I thought I'd leave my raincoat on the banister so I wouldn't forget to take it upstairs."

"Oh." Rollie picked up the liquor bottle. "I'll bring your drink out to you in a minute."

"Okay." Mandy went into the dining room instead of going into the front hall from the kitchen. She picked up the phone book and skimmed the pages until she came to the Ks. There was no Dr. Kramer listed in Noroton. Her heart skipped a beat. Then it occurred to her that her spelling of the name might be wrong. She flipped back the pages to the Cs and found the doctor listed, Cramer, Lewis J., M.D., with his office and house numbers given. That was reassuring in itself. It would be more reassuring to call him and ask about the old lady.

She couldn't do it, of course. Rollie was within earshot in the kitchen, and even if he hadn't been, no doctor would give out information about one of his patients to a complete stranger.

She put down the phone book. She heard Janet coming down the back stairs as she went on into the living room. A moment later, crossing the room, the hallstand mirror brought an eloquent pantomime into her view. Part of the kitchen was reflected in it, the doorway framing Rollie, who stood by the sink with his jaw set in anger. He pushed Janet against the sink and pointed to the dishes in it. Janet shrugged. He slapped her hard across the face. She opened her mouth, but he clapped his hand over it before she could utter a sound. He held her by the arm with his other hand and talked rapidly in an undertone, apparently browbeating her into silence. At last he let her go and both of them moved away from the sink out of range of the mirror. Rollie began a conversation, raising his voice to its normal level.

Mandy slipped across the hall, laid her raincoat on the newel-post and went out onto the front porch, remembering that the screen door had no governor on it and had to be closed gently or it would slam shut.

She moved to the far end of the porch, subduing the impulse to run away as far and fast as she could from the pair inside. She sat down on the railing and tried to collect herself. The scene she had just witnessed in the mirror removed her last doubt that she might be imagining or exaggerating things about the old lady upstairs.

Rollie was no outsider in the plot against her but was taking part in it. Perhaps they had promised him a share of her money.

A gust of wind caught a lock of Mandy's hair and

whipped it across her face. While she was tucking it back into place lightning flashed and was followed by a crash of thunder. As it died away she looked out into the black night with the thought that she had never felt so cut off from people in her life. She wished that she could see a light somewhere.

Her next thought was that she couldn't get on a plane and go home tomorrow. She'd have to go to Bentonville with the Averys and arrange somehow to call Dr. Cramer right away from an outside phone.

In the meantime, the nurse was coming. Her arrival would give the old lady a margin of safety. Nothing could be done to her with a nurse in charge.

Lightning flashed again, blinding Mandy with blue-white light. Then the screen door opened and Rollie appeared with a glass in each hand. Janet was in back of him carrying her own drink.

He gave Mandy her glass and sat down beside her on the railing.

"Thank you," she said, but when she took a sip from it she had to repress a shudder. It was even stronger than the drinks Mr. Avery made.

Janet walked to the edge of the porch, her hand over her hair to protect it from the wind. "God, what a night," she said, her voice almost lost in a volley of thunder.

"Storm's going to break any minute now," Rollie told her and went on to remark that the Averys would be caught in it. Janet said it would probably hold them up getting home.

They spoke matter-of-factly to each other. The violent little scene in the kitchen had been all smoothed over, Mandy thought.

She set her glass down on the railing, tipping it back now and then to let her drink trickle out gradually into the shrubbery. When she raised the glass to her lips she took the smallest possible sips from it.

Janet drew back from a violent burst of thunder and lightning. "Let's go inside," she said. "This is getting to be too much."

"Chicken," Rollie said, but he got to his feet and turned to Mandy. "Pretty windy out here now. Aren't you cold in that sleeveless dress?"

"A little, I guess." She stood up with her glass in her hand. There was nothing left in it but melting ice cubes.

They went indoors. Janet perched on the arm of the sofa and said, "I'd better take a look at Gran as soon as I finish my drink. I hope the storm doesn't wake her up. The way she's been sleeping tonight, that pill I gave her really knocked her out. Or maybe it's because she doesn't feel so hot. She didn't want any supper, but I made her take some tea and toast. Then I gave her another cup of tea before she went to sleep."

Every word she said came from Rollie blatant with his coaching. They didn't know, of course, that Mandy had witnessed what went on between them in the kitchen.

"You'd better take a look at her," Rollie said. "And close the windows while you're up there. It's going to rain like hell before long."

"All right." Janet went upstairs.

Mandy took a last sip of melted ice and set her glass down.

"Let me make you another drink." Rollie got to his feet and picked up his empty glass.

"No, thanks." She felt that she'd had all she could stand of the pair for one evening. She yawned elaborately and looked at her watch. "My lord, it's not eleven o'clock yet and I'm ready to hit my rack. Are you and Janet going to wait up for her parents?"

"Depends on how soon they get here. Maybe we'll just have another drink and rack out ourselves. Sure you won't have one?"

She shook her head and yawned again to soften her refusal. "I'm dead. Good night and thanks a lot for taking me
out to dinner."

"You're welcome. Good night, kid. Sleep tight." Rollie
walked out into the hall with her and then headed for the
kitchen.

Janet, carrying a cup and saucer, was on her way downstairs. "Left these in Gran's room," she said, pausing at the
foot of the staircase with the cup held out in front of her
so that Mandy couldn't miss seeing dregs of tea in it.

This, the girl told herself, was altogether too much. While
she was out on the porch they had poured hot water over a
tea bag and Janet had carried the cup up the back stairs.

"I hope Mother won't be upset that I couldn't get Gran
to eat her supper," Janet continued.

She didn't have any more sense than to embroider on
what was better let alone.

"I wouldn't worry about it," Mandy said.

"What's Rollie doing?"

"Making himself another drink."

"Aren't you going to have one?"

"No, I'm just going to take another look outside and go
to bed."

"Well, Rollie can keep me company while I do the
dishes." Janet turned toward the kitchen. "'Night, Mandy."

"Good night." Mandy watched her walk down the hall,
buttocks moving sinuously from side to side under tight
shorts. As she disappeared into the kitchen she said, "I hope
that's my drink you're making, Rollie. Don't skimp on the
liquor, either. When I drink I like to feel it."

Mandy went to the door and looked out. No rain had
fallen yet, but the storm was almost upon them now in a
tumult of thunder and lightning and wind shrieking
through the branches of the great oak trees on the lawn.

Involuntarily she covered her ears with her hands to shut

out a deafening crash of thunder. Then she opened the door to step out onto the porch.

The cat, crouched on the doormat, shot past her into the house and up the stairs.

13

Mandy's one thought was to catch the cat and put it outside before Rollie discovered that it was in the house.

She snatched up her raincoat—she could roll the cat up in it to avoid being scratched—and ran noiselessly upstairs. At the head of the stairs she came to a halt and looked around her. The bedroom doors were closed. The bathroom door and the door to the ell stood ajar. The cat had gone through one of them. There was no sign of it in the hall.

She tried the bathroom first, getting down on her knees to look under the tub. The cat wasn't there. It was in the ell. If it went down the back stairs and got into the kitchen it would fall into Rollie's hands.

She took off her shoes and went into the ell, leaving the door ajar as she had found it. In her bare feet she moved along the corridor without making a sound. She had cut off almost all of the light from the hall behind her and ahead there was just the feeble light on the back stair landing.

But the cat hadn't gone that far. It was clawing at the old lady's door, mewing to be let in.

Mandy approached it cautiously, holding her breath for fear that she would startle it into making a dash toward the back stairway. But the cat, keeping up its steady plaint, paid no attention to her. It knew where it was, she thought indignantly. It belonged there. It was the old lady's cat. The Averys had tried to drive it away from the house.

She picked it up gently, murmuring reassurances. It struggled furiously at first and raked her arm with its claws before she got it rolled up in the raincoat, leaving its head free. Then she stood for a moment still murmuring to it and rubbing it between the ears. At last the animal lay quiet in the curve of her arm, accepting her ministrations as if it understood that she at least, in this house, was a friend.

She could hear Rollie and Janet talking in the kitchen below, but no sound came from behind the door. Janet must have given her grandmother more than one sleeping pill for her to sleep through the racket of the storm outside.

Mandy listened and rubbed the cat's head harder in her nervousness. Still no sound came from the other side of the door. She began to feel irritated with Janet, who ought to come upstairs again to see if her grandmother was all right. Mandy herself wanted to escape back to her room. There was something frightening about the lack of any sound from the old lady; there was something frightening about the ell itself.

Then, without conscious intent on her part, her hand found the doorknob, turned it and opened the door.

The entry was in darkness, but the lavatory door was open and she could make out the window in line with it. The bedroom door on her right was closed.

Her heart was pounding. Lightning flashed and revealed the telephone stand just as she was about to bump into it. She eased the bedroom door open.

The room was in total darkness, much darker than the entry. She could see nothing at first. She listened for the old lady's breathing but could not hear it. She edged her way over the threshold.

The familiar musty smell of the house greeted her, perhaps a little stronger here than elsewhere. Mingled with it were smells of dust and airlessness. She could sense no other living presence in the room.

The cat fought wildly to free itself. She had to use both hands to hold it. She took a step forward and could make out the footboard of the bed. Then lightning flashed across the bare mattress.

Mandy did not faint from the shock of it but experienced, rather, a feeling of the floor slipping away from her, a moment of suspension of all her faculties. Flattened against the doorjamb, the squirming cat clutched to her, she stood motionless while thunder rolled and echoed and died away. Lightning flashed again across the bare mattress confirming what she had already, unbelievingly, seen.

She caught her breath in what was almost a sob, backed out of the room closing the door after her, and retreated into the corridor. She closed the outer door and ran for the front hall as if toward sanctuary, although none, she knew, existed in this house. She nearly tripped over her discarded shoes, paused to snatch them up and ran still faster as she heard Janet's voice in the hall downstairs.

She was in her bedroom closing the door when the other girl started to climb the stairs. She flew to the front window, unhooked the screen and dropped the cat out onto the porch roof. It would have to find its own way down to the ground. She had no time to think of it now. She had to think of herself, of getting out of here without a moment's delay.

"You in bed already, Mandy?" Janet called from the top of the stairs.

She was in the middle of the room groping for the light cord.

"Just getting ready," she called back and pulled on the light.

She heard Janet go into the ell. She stripped off her dress, threw it on a chair, grabbed her robe from the closet and zipped herself into it. When Janet knocked on her door a minute later she was sitting on the side of her bed brushing her hair. "Come on in," she said.

Janet opened the door but came only a little way into the room. "I thought you were still on the porch," she said. "I was surprised when I looked out and didn't see you."

"I only stayed a minute. I'm awfully tired tonight." Mandy wondered at the normal tone of her voice. She hadn't known if she would be able to speak at all.

"I came up to take a look at Gran."

"How is she?" Mandy forced herself to raise her eyes to Janet's face.

"Still sleeping like a baby. I thought the storm would wake her up by this time."

"Well, you gave her a sleeping pill." Mandy went through the motions of patting back a yawn. "I don't know that the storm will keep me awake either," she said. "I'm simply dead."

"Are you?" Janet's china doll eyes were fixed on her with what seemed to her a peculiar kind of intentness.

"Yes, I really am." Mandy felt suddenly that she couldn't put up with Janet for another second, that there was something so oppressive about her very presence that she couldn't breathe in the same room with her. To hasten her departure she yawned again enormously and said, "I don't know what's doing it. Maybe it was that drink Rollie gave me. He makes them strong enough."

"Yes, maybe that was it. Well, I won't keep you up any longer. 'Night."

"Good night."

Janet went out and closed the door. Mandy didn't move until she heard her going downstairs. Then, as she stood up, she heard what sounded like the light, rapid patter of a small animal's feet running up and down over her head. It took her a moment to realize that it was the first raindrops falling on the roof.

She moved swiftly to the closet and got out a skirt and blouse. She tried to keep her head and think what she would need. Her raincoat—at least it was a break that she'd brought her dark plaid one, not the tan—a scarf to put over her head, her wallet. She'd better wear her sneaks, they'd make no noise.

She put her wallet in her raincoat pocket and laid it on a chair with the skirt and blouse on top of it. She bunched up the bedclothes to make it appear to a casual glance that she was in bed. She put out the light and dressed in the dark, fumbling buttons and zipper in her haste, fighting hysteria.

The stealthy sound of the rain overhead did nothing to calm her, but by the time she was dressed it had quickened into a downpour, lashing against the roof up above and rattling like hailstones on the tin roof of the porch.

It was the final touch, it was just great, she thought, looking out into the pitch-black night. If there were only a light shining somewhere, a single, solitary light—

Forget it, she counseled herself. No matter what the night was like it was better to be out in it than to spend another minute in this house.

She was ready to leave. She opened her door softly and listened. Rollie and Janet were talking in the living room. They had moved in there. She wouldn't be able to slip out the front way.

Halted outside her door she considered her next move.

The porch roof? She doubted that she could get down off it. It was high above the ground, a long way down if she fell. On second thought, she couldn't try it anyway. The living room windows were open. They would surely hear her.

It would have to be the back stairs. She didn't like the idea—she'd have to cut across the corner of the kitchen to the back door and Rollie or Janet might appear while she was doing it—but it was a chance she would have to take.

They were talking in undertones. Was it about how and when they had killed the old lady? Or about how clever they had been, bringing Mandy there to bear witness that she was still alive?

They had made it seem true. How had they worked it?

There would be time to think about it later.

She went on silent feet into the ell, not looking, as she passed it, at the door in the corridor that opened on the center, the focal point of the evil she had sensed in the house.

The storm, now at its height, would have drowned out any slight sounds she made, but she tried to make none.

She went down the back stairway. She was reaching out her hand to open the door at the foot of the stairs when she heard Mr. Avery come into the kitchen from the outside and call, "Well, here we are."

She hadn't heard the car arrive over the noise of the storm. Another moment and she would have opened the door and walked right into him. And Mrs. Avery, who came in next.

She retreated up a few steps, poised for flight and then stopped to listen.

Someone came from the front of the house. It was Rollie. "So you're back," he said, "and everything went off smoothly."

"Without a hitch," Mr. Avery replied. He lowered his voice. "Where's Mandy?"

"Asleep in her bed."

"Good."

They wanted her in bed out of the way.

Where was Janet? She was wearing sneaks so that Mandy wouldn't be apt to hear her if she came out into the kitchen. She wasn't inclined to exert herself, though, and might very well be stretched out on the living room sofa with the front door in view.

For that matter, was Mrs. Avery still in the kitchen? Mandy hadn't heard her speak yet. Then there was the nurse—no, of course there wasn't one. The old lady was dead, past the need of her.

Only an hour ago Rollie had said the nurse was coming and must have had a story ready to explain her nonappearance. She would never appear, but she had played a role in making Mandy believe that the old lady was still alive.

What had they done with her body?

Never mind that now, she would think about it later. Now she had to concentrate on getting them all located before she made a move toward the front door.

A chair scraped across the floor. Rollie said, "Well, put the bag on the table so I can get a look."

"Wait a minute." It was Mr. Avery's voice. "Evelyn, shut the back door and lock it. Better shut the hall door too, and pull down the shades."

Mrs. Avery, then, was still in the kitchen. Mandy could hear her moving around closing doors and drawing the shades.

She was cut off from escape the back way. If they moved into the living room she would be cut off from the front door too.

No use worrrying about it. If it happened, she'd just have to find another way out of the house. She couldn't go back to her room and wait until they were all in bed and asleep. She would go to pieces. She was on the edge of it now.

Where was Janet? She must have stayed in the living room or she would have taken some part in the conversation by this time. Perhaps she had. Mandy couldn't hear everything that was said. The storm was making too much noise. Right now, for example, they were talking about money, but she could only catch a few words here and there.

Then Rollie's voice rose exultantly. "Just look at it," he exclaimed. "Never saw so much in my whole life."

There was money in the bag the Averys had brought back from Bentonville or wherever they went. It was the old lady's money, of course. She hadn't, after all, hidden it in the house, but they had somehow found out where it was.

It had nothing to do with Mandy. It was Janet who concerned her. Was she still in the living room, or hanging over Rollie's chair blinking her china doll eyes at the money?

It was nerve-racking not to know. But it wasn't just the suspense that had her shaking from head to foot, she knew. It was dread of making her move. She might even be using Janet's whereabouts as an excuse to postpone it.

She mustn't wait any longer, though. It was difficult to judge the progress of the storm, shut up as she was on the stairway, but it seemed to have passed its peak. She didn't want that. She had better take her chances now on Janet's whereabouts before it died away completely. She was counting on it to cover up any sound she might make getting out of the house.

She moved up cautiously to the next stair and then checked herself as she heard Mrs. Avery ask, "Are you sure she took it?" and Rollie's reply. "Of course I am," he said. "I put it in her drink and it began to take effect right away. It made her so sleepy she couldn't wait to get to bed."

They were talking about her. Rollie had tried to drug her.

A clap of thunder drowned out whatever was said next. Mandy couldn't have followed it, anyway. She clung to the stair rail for support, saying over and over under her breath, "Thank God I didn't drink it. Oh, thank God, thank God . . ."

As the thunder rolled off into silence she heard Mr. Avery's voice. ". . . another half hour so she's sound asleep. It'll make it easier all around."

Make what easier?

She scarcely listened to Rollie's statements that half an

hour was the outside limit, that they had plenty of things to do and he had to get out of there sometime tonight.

Things to do. . . . Get rid of the old lady's body tonight while Mandy lay in drugged sleep? Where was it now? Down cellar or out in the barn?

No, the girl thought suddenly, that wasn't what they were talking about. Sometime since the nurse left Saturday they had killed the old lady, but she had no part in their plans for tonight. Those plans were centered on Mandy herself; they had tried to drug her because it would make it easier to carry them out.

Make what easier?

Her very bones knew the answer: easier to kill her.

Never mind why; that was what they meant to do.

Her legs gave way. She sat down on the stair fighting for breath against suffocating terror.

The next thing she heard was Mr. Avery's voice. "Let's just make sure she's asleep," he said.

"Don't look at me." It was Janet who spoke. "I'm not going near her again. It gives me the creeps. I've had them all day. Don't worry, though, that she's still awake. I was up there like about ten minutes ago and she was yawning her head off then."

"I'll go up and take a look at her just the same," Mrs. Avery said.

Strength flowed back into Mandy and brought her instantly to her feet. She skimmed the stairs and moved without a sound in the corridor. Her goal was the front stairs and she had a good head start, she thought, on Mrs. Avery. She didn't have to think about the others for the moment. They were in the kitchen with the hall door shut. Before Mrs. Avery could get to Mandy's room from the ell she would be out the front door and away.

She automatically associated Mrs. Avery with the back stairs, but as she darted out of the ell she heard a door open below and someone come into the front hall from the kitchen. Mrs. Avery, going up to check on Mandy, was using the front stairs.

Mandy tore into her room and shut the door. She whipped off her scarf and had just time to get into bed and pull the covers up to her chin when the door opened. Mrs. Avery came into the room and halted beside the bed.

Mandy watched her from under her lashes, trying to breathe slowly and evenly as if asleep. But she had no control over her heartbeat. It sounded so loud that it must be heard.

Mrs. Avery stood looking down at her. A faceless figure silhouetted against the hall light, she seemed taller than she was and terrifying.

This was the mother of her pen pal of many years' standing, the woman who wrote gay, friendly little messages to them on her Christmas cards each year. This was the woman Mandy's mother had chatted with pleasantly on the phone just last Thursday when she called her to verify the arrangements for Mandy's visit.

Now, less than a week later, this same woman stood over her bed satisfying herself that Mandy had fallen into a drugged sleep that would make it easier to kill her.

In a corner of her mind the girl still rejected what was going on. It was too unbelievable; it couldn't be true.

She moaned and moved her head. It wouldn't do to have Mrs. Avery report back downstairs that she was already so deep in sleep that their project of murder could be carried out without further delay.

After a last look at her Mrs. Avery withdrew as quietly as she had entered.

Mandy was out of the bed before she was halfway down the stairs and in another moment had her door open, waiting for the older woman to get back to the kitchen.

"She's asleep but still mumbling a little," Mandy heard her say. "We'd better give her a few minutes more."

They weren't hardened killers—they were squeamish enough to want her sound asleep before they came near her.

How were they going to do it? Strangle her? Smother her? Or were they going to use a knife?

She mustn't think about that. She was close to panic as it was.

"I could do with a drink while we're waiting," she heard Mr. Avery say. "Anyone else care for one?"

"Make them all around," Mrs. Avery said.

Mandy heard the refrigerator door open and close as she advanced to the head of the stairs. She paused there for a moment. Weren't they going to shut the door into the hall?

No one bothered to. She was supposed to be in a drugged sleep.

Her heart almost failed her at the thought of getting down the stairs with the door open on the Averys only a few feet away. But she had no choice. She would just have to be as quiet as she could on the creaky old stairs. She started down them keeping close to the wall.

Conversation in the kitchen helped to cover up the faint sounds she made. Then a faucet was turned on and ice cubes rattled in the sink, which helped still more. While the water was running she rushed down the last few steps and slid past the parlor doors well out of the path of light from the kitchen.

The water was turned off just as she reached the screen door. A sudden lull settled over the group at the same moment. The only sound was the clink of ice cubes being dropped into glasses.

Her nerves keyed to an almost unbearable pitch, Mandy waited for someone to break the silence. She didn't trust the rusty hinges on the screen door not to make a noise that would be heard in the kitchen unless there was conversation to cover it up.

She looked out into the night. A flash of lightning from far off gave her a glimpse of the road that would lead her to safety. Thunder rumbled in the distance but the wind had dropped and the rain, although still coming down hard, was no longer a downpour. The storm was nearly over, its fury spent.

The blackness of the night held no terrors for her. All that she asked at the moment was to vanish into it.

Rollie broke the silence in the kitchen. "Well, drinks coming up," he said. "Anyone got a toast to suggest?"

Mandy pushed the screen door open a few inches. A faint squeak came from it.

"I'll offer a toast," Mr. Avery said. "Here's to a clean getaway tomorrow."

She opened the door a little wider and edged through it.

The cat was her undoing. She had forgotten its existence since she had put it out on the roof but it was back on the doormat. She stepped squarely on it, was thrown off-balance, and pulled at the door to save herself from falling. The cat yowled and darted off the porch. The door slipped out of Mandy's grasp and slammed shut.

14

"My God, what was that?" someone in the kitchen exclaimed.

She went flying down the steps. Instinct sent her around the corner of the house without the loss of a moment to consider which way she should go. Her original plan of heading for the road was out of the question. The lawn was too open and the road itself, if she ever reached it, offered no concealment. It seemed to her that her best chance lay in getting across the field in back of the house and over the stone wall into the patch of woods beyond it.

The screen door was flung open behind her. She heard Rollie call, "Janet, run upstairs and check on Mandy. Art, take a look out back and see if anyone's around."

Her feet seemed winged carrying her out around the barrier of shrubbery and on past the ell. She was nearing the grape arbor when Janet threw open the corridor window and yelled out, "Mandy's gone."

Alarmingly close behind her, Rollie yelled back, "She can't be far away. Get the flashlight from my car. Get Steve's too. Somebody drive out to the road and see if she went that way."

She cut through the grape arbor and tried to run still faster. She heard a car start up, headed for the road. A tumult of voices shouting directions and counterdirections arose in the yard behind her.

Suddenly the ground became bumpy and rough beneath her feet with long wet grass catching at her ankles. She had reached the field. The footing was slippery, but she dared not slow down. When she glanced back over her shoulder she was dismayed that she wasn't farther away from the house.

The flashlights were her greatest worry. She tried to think ahead as she ran. She would gain all the distance she could and then, if they came into the field with them, she would lie flat on the ground. Hummocks and depressions would give her some cover while she worked her way to the wall.

Her plan was barely made when a flash of lightning betrayed her. She threw herself down, but it was too late. A shout from Rollie told her she had been spotted.

She would never get away from them now. In despair she lay for a moment panting for breath. Then she was up again running in a lateral direction away from where they had seen her. She ran for a few hundred feet before fear of another flash of lightning made her drop to the ground again.

Feet pounded into the field, a flashlight bobbing ahead. She began to crawl farther away from it, although she knew from what she had noticed of the field by daylight that it would do her no good. She had turned in the wrong direction. The field was fairly open if she had run the opposite way, but at this end it was hemmed in by a dense thicket of overgrown barberry bushes that ran from the road past the house to the stone wall. She would make so much noise trying to get through it—if she could get through it at all—that she would be caught immediately.

When she got her breath back she would have to think of something else.

The car came back up the driveway. There were shouts from Mr. Avery to drive it up on the lawn and point the headlights toward the field. He cursed and commanded as the car was maneuvered back and forth but to no avail. There were trees in the way of bringing it up close to the house and when it was finally parked any glow from the headlights that might have reached the field was completely cut off by the shrubbery on the side lawn.

"Leave them on anyway, Flo," Mr. Avery shouted. "And hurry up with that flashlight in the glove compartment."

They were calling each other by different names. The thought barely slid into Mandy's mind and out again.

Rollie, circling the area around him with his flashlight, was moving toward the stone wall.

Mr. Avery came toward the field with the other flashlight, shouting back, "Flo, shut off that motor and take the keys out of the car. Barbara, quit poking around and get the keys out of Regan's car. We don't want her circling back to them."

Rollie called to him, "She's trying to get to the woods, Steve. God, we'll never find her if she makes it."

"She'll never make it." Mr. Avery's reply came confidently.

He was right, Mandy thought in a fresh burst of terror. The woods were as far out of her reach as the red brick house in Connecticut or the cottage in Maine. Both places were home to her but home was a word she mustn't think about. It might make her cry and if she ever started—

Lightning flashed again. She tried to burrow into the ground. It didn't matter, she told herself, that it was a weak flash, the last gasp, so to speak, of the storm. Any flash at all would betray her if she got up and ran.

She heard Mrs. Avery and Janet come into the field. They had no flashlights. She couldn't see them.

Mr. Avery and Rollie met in the middle of the field. Rollie took charge. "We'll begin at the stone wall and work back from it," he said.

She missed Mr. Avery's reply.

"Quarter the field . . . four of us and only one of her," was the next thing she heard.

Mr. Avery, his flashlight probing the darkness ahead of him, moved diagonally toward the stone wall at Mandy's end of the field.

Mrs. Avery and Janet advanced into the field, coming within range of Rollie's flashlight. Mandy caught a word here and there as he gave them quick instructions. The barn and thicket were mentioned, the edge of the field.

She filled in the gaps herself. Mrs. Avery and Janet were to patrol the edge of the field between the barn and the thicket.

They melted back into the darkness as Rollie turned toward the stone wall. Then Mandy heard him call to them over his shoulder, "Remember now, keep quiet, keep your eyes and ears peeled for the least sound or movement."

The flashlights began to range back and forth along the wall, nowhere near her as yet but gradually coming nearer.

She had to do something. She couldn't just lie here in a paralysis of fear until they caught her.

Some small creature brushed against her outstretched hand. A mouse, a toad? She smothered a cry.

She heard Mrs. Avery and Janet whisper to each other, one of them not very far away from her, but when she raised her head, straining to see them, they remained invisible in the dark.

If she couldn't see them, they couldn't see her. A plan took shape in her mind. While they searched for her in the field she would head back toward the house. Mrs. Avery and Janet had a lot of ground to cover, well over two hundred feet of it, in their patrol. She would try to slip between them.

Flat on the ground, using her arms for leverage, Mandy began to pull herself toward them, the steady fall of rain covering the slight sounds she made.

Rollie and Mr. Avery, although taking their time, ranging far and wide with their flashlights, were not so far away as they had been a minute ago.

Janet complained in a whisper sibilantly clear that she was getting drenched to the skin and would just have to run back to the house for her raincoat.

"You'll do nothing of the kind," Mrs. Avery retorted in a fierce whisper. "Shut up now. Keep moving and keep your eyes and ears open."

From the direction of their voices Mandy judged that they were forty to fifty feet away from her and that she was about midway between them.

Slowly and carefully she continued to pull herself forward. But when she looked back panic seized her. The flashlights seemed perilously close; in no time at all they would begin to lighten the blackness around her. Already she thought that she could almost make out movement ahead of her.

Should she get up and make a run for it?

She couldn't. She would be seen. They would catch her.

They would catch her anyway at her present snail's pace.

She began to steel herself to try it. Mrs. Avery's voice had come from her right, Janet's from her left. She changed direction toward Janet, the less alert of the two, she thought, the one she would have a better chance of eluding.

It was all very well to make the decision to get up and run for it, but it was another thing, she discovered, to do it. She found herself hugging the ground for the illusion of safety it gave her.

She had to get up—

Her hands tightened around a clump of grass.

"Steve! Regan!" It was Mrs. Avery's voice. "Turn off the flashlights. There's a car coming."

Mandy saw it then, the glow of distant headlights reflected in the sky.

The flashlights were turned off. Stygian darkness settled on the field.

It was now or never.

She got to her feet. She wouldn't have to run. The unexpected boon of darkness favored a less hazardous course. Crouched almost double to stay as close to the ground as possible, she moved lightly on the balls of her feet. (Shades of Miss Knight and her long-ago ballet lessons: "Remember, girls, we bend our knees, we come down lightly, we are little fairies, not great elephants lumbering over Africa.")

That's what she was, a little fairy, treading lightly, lightly, knees bent. Her head must be light, too, or was she going nuts? (Miss Knight, this wasn't quite what you had in mind, was it, with your glissades and tour jetés and arabesques?)

Smoother ground at last, the lawn beneath her feet. She had passed safely between Mrs. Avery and Janet.

But now the car that had been her salvation for the moment became a source of danger to her, so close to the house that its lights shone on the roof.

She dropped down and lay flat on the ground again, motionless until the car went by—slowing down a little as if the driver was casting a curious glance at Mr. Avery's car parked on the lawn with its lights shining on the front of the house.

After it had passed she got up and ran into the grape arbor and pressed herself in among the leaves. The flash-lights were turned on again in the field. But she had gained a breathing space, time to think about what she should do next.

Exhausted, chilled through from her soggy wet clothes, Mandy tried to bring her mind to bear on her total situation. So far, as one shock followed upon the other, she had been making hand-to-mouth moves, a series of them that had got her out of the house, and then, when the cat had ruined her escape, a fresh series that had taken her into the field and back to her present temporary refuge.

What was her next move to be? She looked around her. Mr. Avery's car lights were an effective barrier in front of the house. They not only blocked her off from the road but cast a diffused glow over the whole area. There was every chance that she would be silhouetted against it even lying on the ground, if she tried to get across the lawn on this side of the house.

What about the other side, though? She looked out from

the end of the arbor and shook her head. The nearest
shelter, a considerable distance away, was the shed in back
of the house. To reach it she would have to cross a stretch
of lawn that seemed anything but safe, with light spilling
over it through the cracked shades on the kitchen windows.
She would pay with her life for the least forgetfulness of
the fact that the Averys, whenever they glanced toward the
house, were looking from a dark area into a brighter one.

They were growing impatient, almost frantic out there in
the field, flashlights swooping in wider and wider arcs almost back to the edge of it, Janet calling out something
on a whining note, Rollie, with grim fury, shutting her up.

Mandy told herself that she had to make some sort of a
move right away but didn't see how she could escape on
her own. One against four, she was in desperate need of
help.

In the back of her mind, from the moment she began
to take stock of her situation, she had known what she
would have to do.

She couldn't face it, though. Every nerve and muscle in
her body shrank from going back into the house. She would
stay right where she was. If she got under the bench and
pulled the vines down over her they'd never find her.

Wouldn't they? When they gave up searching the field
they would turn their flashlights into every nook and cranny
of the yard. The grape arbor would be one of the first
places they'd look. She had to get out of it this very minute.

She ran to the evergreens, keeping the arbor between her
and the field. Then she lay down and wriggled her way
through a tangle of trailing branches, scarcely aware of
sharp needles that scratched her face and hands and
caught in her hair. She emerged from under them at the
corner of the front porch with the car lights, appallingly
bright, shining in her eyes.

It had all been for nothing, she thought, looking up at

the house. She was right back where she had started from ten or fifteen minutes ago. Or was it twenty minutes ago, or even longer? Or had there ever been a time when she wasn't being hunted?

She checked this train of thought instantly. Self-pity could come later. There wasn't time for it now.

She ran up the porch steps. The cat, stubbornly, was back on the doormat, but she was gentle in pushing it away with her foot. She bore it no malice. Although it had brought her disaster, it had saved her in the first place by taking her into the ell.

Now she was on her way back to the ell. She went over the threshold into the silent house swallowing hard on a sudden wave of nausea.

Nothing was changed. The dim light in the hall still burned, a lamp in the living room was still turned on.

She ran up the stairs. The door to the ell stood open. Cool fresh air blew through the corridor from the window Janet had flung wide to announce that Mandy was gone.

She opened the door to the entry and was a little startled to find that it wasn't nearly as dark as it had been earlier when there had been no light coming through the lavatory window from the yard below. Then she realized that Rollie's car lights were turned on to keep her away from the field on that side of the house. She could not have got across it unseen. There had been no choice for her but the one she had made.

She tried not to look at the bedroom door, the door to the chamber of horrors, but there it was, a blank surface that made her flesh creep.

She turned to the telephone, but before she could pick up the receiver a sudden commotion outside sent her flying to the corridor window. Mr. Avery had found the place where she had started to pull herself along the ground and was following the trail of flattened grass she had left behind her, shouting to the others to stand clear of it. In a moment or two it would bring them all back into the yard.

She ran to the telephone, picked up the receiver and dialed the operator.

The number rang twice. Then a brisk pleasant voice said, "Operator."

Mandy choked up at the sound of it, an avenue to help, to life itself.

"Operator," the voice repeated patiently.

"Please—" She cleared her throat and got herself under some semblance of control. "Please get the police for me right away."

"The police? I'll connect you with—"

"No, no, there isn't time. Call them and tell them to come right away."

"Can you tell me what the trouble is?"

"I'm sorry but it would take too long. If they don't come immediately—" her voice broke. "Please—"

The operator, sensing her youth and her terror, said, "All right, dear. I'll get them there as fast as I can. Just give me your name and address."

"My name is Amanda O'Brien but I don't live in Noroton. I've been visiting here at a Mrs. Johnson's house. There's no street address. It's about seven or eight miles from the center on a country road going toward Route 11.

"What's the phone number?"

"I don't know." Mandy couldn't hold back a sob. "And I don't dare turn on a light to find out."

"Well, don't worry about it. We can check it here."

"It's a big old house on the right-hand side of the road as you come from the center of Noroton. It's all by itself with no other—just a minute—" Mandy put down the phone and ran to the window. Lights flashed below. They had lost her trail at the edge of the field and were trying to pick it up in the yard.

She ran back to the phone and said in a hurried under-tone, "I can't talk any longer. They're right outside the house now. Just get the police right away and tell them—" She hesitated, knowing how melodramatic her next state-ment would sound, but then it burst out of her. "Tell them these people are trying to kill me," she said and hung up.

15

When Mandy got back to the corridor window Rollie was sending Mrs. Avery around on the other side of the house to look for her. "Don't forget the shed," he said. "The rest of the buildings too. She could be hiding anywhere. Barbara, you start looking in the shrubbery while I look under the front porch."

Mandy lost sight of them as they started their search of the yard. There was no sign of Mr. Avery. Where was he? Making his way silently into the house?

She whirled around toward the back stairs, thinking that she heard a tread creak. Then she relaxed as a car started in front of the house. Mr. Avery was accounted for.

Presently the car came into view moving slowly, its lights on high beam supplemented by a flashlight that swung back and forth over the fields on both sides of the road.

Standing at the window she pushed back a wet strand of hair from her face and for the first time became aware of how much her hands hurt. She touched one with the other tentatively. They were covered with cuts and scratches she couldn't remember getting.

She saw the car turn around and head back, the flashlight still circling over the fields.

"Steve's not having any luck either." Janet's voice came from the shrubbery below the window.

"I told him it was a waste of time," Rollie replied sharply as he moved toward the grape arbor with his flashlight. "She never made the road. She's right around here somewhere and we've got to find her."

The car, nearing the house, moved out of Mandy's range of vision. She ran to the lavatory window and caught sight of it again going on up the road, the flashlight swinging back and forth as Mr. Avery continued his search for her in that direction.

Then she saw Mrs. Avery, who came around the corner of the barn and cut across the yard toward the back of the house. Mandy, trying to keep track of everyone's where-abouts, ran back to the window in the corridor.

She could hear Janet moving around off to her left but couldn't see her. Rollie was at the far side of the lawn probing the thicket with his flashlight. He turned swiftly as Mrs. Avery called to him almost from under the window.

"What are you doing here?" he demanded, running over to her. "Go back where you were and keep on looking for Mandy."

"I've looked everywhere for her already. There's not a sign of her. She's gone, Regan. She got away somehow while we were still out in the field. We'll never find her now and we'd better get away ourselves while we can."

"You can at least keep an eye on the kitchen door. If she's hiding in the house we don't want her getting out while you stand here yakking."

"She's not in it," Mrs. Avery protested. "It's the last place she'd head for."

They had thought of the house. Mandy's heart leaped with fright. All her terror, eased a little since she had made the phone call, came surging back.

They hadn't thought of the phone, though, she told her-self. Not yet, in the hectic rush of their search for her.

"That's right." Janet's voice. She came around the shrub-bery. "You wouldn't catch me going near the house if I was in Mandy's shoes."

"I told you to stay out in front," Rollie snapped at her.

The front door was unguarded for the moment. If she could get out that way—Mandy ran into the front hall—

she could find a hiding place that had already been searched.

She stopped short at the head of the stairs. Someone had turned on the porch light.

When she got back to the window Janet was asking Rollie why they couldn't search the house right now and get it over with.

"Goddammit, I told you why before," he retorted. "If she's in there we've got her trapped, but if she's hiding somewhere in the yard she's just waiting for us to go inside so she can get away. Now both of you go back where you belong. We'll keep looking for her out here until Steve gets back. My God, don't you people realize that we're going to be on the run for the rest of our lives if she lives to tell her story?"

"You don't have to remind me of it," Mrs. Avery said in a tone sharp with anxiety. "I've been thinking about it every minute that we've been looking for her."

A moment later she was gone. Then Janet and Rollie separated. She went back toward the front of the house and he began to move around the yard, turning his flashlight in all directions.

Mandy's gaze followed him. He had said ". . . if she lives to tell her story."

She had known all along that they meant to kill her, but somehow it became more of a reality, more monstrous put into words.

They were a nest of monsters, Mr. and Mrs. Avery, Janet and Rollie.

Only now they were calling each other by different names. . . .

Never mind about that. She had to find a place to hide until the police got there. How long would it take them? Fifteen or twenty minutes, perhaps.

How many minutes had gone by since she had talked

to the operator? At least five, although it was hard to tell at a time like this how long a minute lasted. All she could be sure of was that she had to find a place to hide until the police arrived.

Where? Under the old lady's bed in that awful room across the corridor?

Calm down and think.

Her own room, four walls and a closet, offered nothing. Janet's was the same. She would take a look at the other two bedrooms, but there was no reason to think that they would offer more.

Somewhere downstairs? How would she get down there? Not by the back way into the lighted kitchen; not by the front stairs, either, with Janet on guard outside.

The attic—was there one? Well, there were slits of windows under the roof so there must be some sort of a space up above with a stairway to it.

But even as she thought of it Mandy was rejecting the thought, knowing that she could never make herself go up into the darkness of a totally strange place with no way of finding out what concealment, if any, it would afford her. All too easily, she could be cornered up there.

She went to the front part of the house and looked at the two bedrooms she hadn't seen. They were as barren of hiding places as her own room and Janet's. A chain hanging from a trapdoor in Rollie's closet showed her the way to the space, the rat-in-a-trap space, up above. She shuddered and turned away from it.

Back in the ell she stood facing the old lady's door. She couldn't go into that room to see what it offered, couldn't even open the door. Yes, she could—she had to. It was just a door that led into an empty room.

Her body, trembling from head to foot, didn't agree.

She took hold of the doorknob, hesitated.

What if the old lady's body was under the bed?

It wasn't. Of course it wasn't.

Her flesh crept in disagreement, but she opened the door and went into the room.

Light came in the two windows from Rollie's car outside. A glance revealed the layout and furniture. Four bare walls, a bureau as bare as the mattress on the wooden bed; a straight chair, a huge old wardrobe with what looked like a small suitcase on top of it. No closet. If there had ever been one, it had become part of the lavatory and entry.

On her way to the wardrobe Mandy stopped at the bed and looked under it. The old lady's body wasn't there. Nothing was there but dust stirred up by her breath. The whole room smelt of it.

How recently had the old lady occupied it? They had stripped it since her death, but when had they killed her?

Mandy opened the wardrobe door. It was empty.

The room offered no more prospect of concealment than the others.

Could she lock herself in and barricade the door?

There was no key in the lock. She couldn't budge the wardrobe or the heavy wooden bed. The bureau was too easy to move, too small and light to make any sort of a barricade against two men.

Where was she going to hide? Her glance ranged over the room despairingly. Any minute now they would come inside and start to look for her. It would be utterly ironic if she were to get herself murdered for lack of some corner where she could hide until the police arrived.

She heard a car in the driveway. The back porch roof cut off her view of it. Hope flaring, she ran into the lavatory and looked out the window. But it was only Mr. Avery returning from his fruitless quest.

As he got out of his car Rollie appeared from in back of the house and Mrs. Avery came down the back porch steps to join them.

Mandy tested the window. It stuck for a moment. She worked at it until she could raise it a couple of inches. Then she knelt down to listen to what seemed to be an argument below.

Rollie's voice, quick and assertive, was the first to reach her. "We're not leaving until we've searched the house from cellar to attic," he said. "Steve, we'd better take the downstairs and let Flo and Barbara do the upstairs. They might not be able to stop her if she's inside and makes a break for one of the doors."

"I'll tell you where she is," Mrs. Avery put in acidly. "If she isn't waking up the people in the nearest house right now, she will be in the next few minutes. I say we should grab the money and run before we have the police on our necks."

"Here comes a car," Mr. Avery said. "Turn off your lights, Regan, and let's get inside and shut the doors. It's almost midnight. We don't want anyone getting nosy about us."

Rollie turned off his car lights. Janet from the corner of the house, called to him, "When in the hell are we going to scram out of here?"

"Go in the front door and make sure you close it. And get the lead out. There's a car coming."

The police? Hope glued Mandy to the window even though she heard them all coming into the house. But the car went by.

What was keeping the police? Had the operator got them so mixed up that they couldn't find the house?

Of course not. She had sounded very competent. They just hadn't had time to get here yet.

Mandy made a silent retreat into the bedroom. The only protection she could think of for herself was to wedge the chair under the doorknob and push the bureau up against it. Perhaps she would even be able to move the bed once she stopped being careful not to make any noise. She had no idea of how long it would keep them out, but at least long enough, she thought, for her to get the message across to them that she had called the police.

She could hear voices and movement below her in the kitchen and footsteps on the cellar stairs. The search of the house had begun.

She closed the bedroom door and leaned against it for a moment, courage draining away.

But she had no time to indulge a mood brought on by fear and exhaustion. She had to get ready to make her last stand. Like Custer, she told herself grimly. Both against savages.

The chair stood between the windows. Her heart sank as she picked it up. It seemed too flimsy to hold the door at all.

She had nothing else.

Turning toward the door with it her glance fell on the porch roof outside the windows. Would Mrs. Avery and Janet look out there? They were wildly impatient to get away and would rush through their search of the upstairs. They might not even think of the roof.

She set the chair down and went to the windows. The first one she tried was stuck fast, but the other was so loose in its frame that it rattled when she pushed it up.

She heard footsteps on the front stairs. She must make her choice.

The flimsiness of the chair made it for her. She put it back in place, crawled out the window and closed it gently after her.

She lay down on her side, raincoat wrapped tight around her, back pressed against the wall. She had done what she could for herself. All that was left was to pray as she had never prayed before in her life. She prayed that they wouldn't find her; she prayed that the police would come.

The rain had stopped and she could hear water dripping

from the eaves. But no sounds of the search reached her. In the quiet of the night it almost seemed removed from her, a thing apart, until the bedroom door opened. She heard voices then through the loose-fitting window, Janet's first, loud with irritation, "—crazy, if you ask me," and Mrs. Avery's reply: "We'll be finished in a minute."

The next moment the light came on, so shockingly bright to Mandy that it didn't seem possible that it could come from a bulb of the same dim kind as the others in the house.

She shut her eyes tight against it and tried to become part of the unyielding wall at her back, expecting each moment to hear one of them cry, "There she is on the roof."

The cry didn't come. She opened her eyes and saw that only the outer half of the roof caught the light. It came nowhere near her; she lay in deep shadow.

She heard the wardrobe door open and close. Janet said, "Well, she's not in here or anywhere else in the house. She never was, but you couldn't tell Regan that."

"Let's get out of here," Mrs. Avery said. "Oh, the roof. I'll just take a look. Not that she's out there."

Mandy stopped breathing entirely, or thought she did. But it was the other window that Mrs. Avery went to, her shadow moving ahead of her on the roof. She scarcely took the time to give it a cursory glance before she said, "She's not out there," and turned away.

The light went out and they left the room, not bothering to close the door.

In the shielding dark Mandy dared to breathe again and then to ease her rigid body, rolling over on her stomach to take her weight off her arm. The hammering of her heart began to lessen. They hadn't found her. In a few minutes they would give up and go away.

She would stay right where she was, though, until the

police arrived, just in case their departure might be a trick to lure her out of hiding.

The kitchen door opened and Rollie's voice, sharp with anger, came up to her. "I don't give a good goddamn what you left upstairs, Barbara, we're getting out of here right now."

Janet's voice, sullen with resentment: "You weren't in such a great big hurry when you made us waste all that time searching the house."

"Shut up and get moving. Flo, forget about the lights. What difference do they make?"

Clatter of feet on the steps; Rollie asking who had the money, Mr. Avery replying that he had it; then the decision to leave the Renault behind, taking just Mr. Avery's car.

The doors opened and slammed shut, Mandy counting one, two, three, four as all of them got into it. The motor started, the lights came on. In another moment they would be gone. . . .

But the car faced the barn. As it was backed around its lights swept the roof well past the edge, so close that if Mandy had stretched out her hand it would have come within their arc.

Had they seen her? She thought not at first. Then the car, headed down the driveway, stopped and backed up.

They had seen her—at least seen something—that one of them had had a delayed reaction to; perhaps she had been seen as a dark blob on the roof.

That was what she had come to—a blob on the roof. She had nowhere to hide, no resources left except to lie motionless where she was.

A car door opened. Footsteps in the yard, on the porch. Rollie's voice: "I know just where it is; it won't take me a minute."

False note in the voice, note of the hunter trying to lull his prey.

Stealthy footsteps below; Mr. Avery, slipping out of the car in case Rollie needed him.

Still she didn't move, hoping against hope, against reason, against instinct that had turned her body to ice.

Dead silence, almost unendurable, shattered by the bedroom window going up with a bang. Rollie, framed in it, said, "So there you are, Mandy," and threw one leg over the sill.

She sprang to her feet and backed away toward the edge of the roof. "Don't you touch me," she cried. "Don't you dare! I've called the police. They'll be here any minute."

He made no answer. He came out onto the roof in a boxer's crouch.

"Go away!" She took another step backward. "You try to grab me and I'll pull you off the roof with me. Go away! The police—"

Still he was silent. He circled out around her, moving warily, mindful of her threat to pull him off the roof with her. The car lights threw his shadow, distorted and thickened, against the wall. He held his hands in front of him, palms out.

In a frenzy of terror she divined his intent: to come at her in a rush and push her off the roof. She screamed and veered toward the open window.

"Christ, shut her up, there's a car coming," Mr. Avery shouted from below.

Out of the tail of her eye Mandy saw him run to his car. The car lights went out. In the sudden darkness she flung herself headlong through the open window. She landed on all fours, scrambled to her feet, spun around and slammed the window on Rollie's hands. His yell of pain and rage followed her as she fled the room. She had a head start on him and held it in the corridor and in a mad rush down the stairs. He gained on her when she had to stop to open the front door and was right on her heels as she streaked off the porch. The next moment he caught her.

She screamed and fought until he pinned her arms to her side in an iron grip from behind, clamped his free hand over her mouth and dragged her back into the shrubbery to wait for the approaching car to go by.

When it turned in at the driveway Mr. Avery was just rounding the corner of the house to come to Rollie's aid and Mandy was still struggling to free herself. The headlights caught them, frozen for a timeless moment in a tableau that needed no words to make its meaning clear.

At the eleventh hour the police had arrived.

16

The tableau broke. Mr. Avery darted back around the corner, Rollie hurled Mandy aside and ran the other way.

An officer with drawn gun leaped out of the cruiser before it had come to a stop shouting at Rollie, "Halt!"

He kept running, following the route Mandy herself had taken out around the shrubbery toward the field in back of the house. The pursuing officer fired a warning shot over his head and when it was ignored, took aim, missed him with the second shot and brought him down with the third.

On the other side of the house Mr. Avery was gunning the motor of his car into life before the cruiser had come to a full stop. Skidding on the wet grass he speeded out over the lawn trying to bypass the cruiser.

He had no chance of making it. Two more officers poured out of the cruiser shooting at his tires. The car slewed around, almost turned over and came to a screeching halt.

"All right," one of the officers shouted. "Everybody out with their hands up."

No one, at the moment, had time to spare for Mandy. She had fallen face down when Rollie hurled her aside and at first, lying in a heap, she made no effort to get back up on her feet. Indeed, as reaction set in, safety attained after mortal danger, she felt as if she had turned into jelly and would never be able to move again.

She kept track, though, of what was going on: Rollie, a bullet in his leg, hobbling back to the house, the officer who had shot him supporting most of his weight and lowering him to the top step of the porch; the others climbing out of the car, hands in the air, Janet sobbing protests that she hadn't done anything and that none of it was her fault.

At last one of the officers came over to Mandy from the cruiser. "Are you hurt, miss?" he asked.

She shook her head.

He helped her to her feet. "Sure you're all right?"

"Yes, quite sure." She was almost abrupt, afraid that she would break down, make an exhibition of herself in front of her rescuers.

"Good. Are you Amanda O'Brien, the girl who called?"

"Yes."

His glance went over her, taking in pallor, scratches, bedraggled clothes, general dishevelment. "You look as if you've had a pretty rough time."

She managed a smile. "At least I'm all in one piece."

"Well, yes." He smiled back at her and then spoke to the officer standing guard over Rollie. "This looks too complicated for a radio call," he said. "I'll go inside and phone headquarters for assistance."

"Okay, Sergeant."

He was a sergeant. Mandy hadn't noticed the stripes on his sleeves.

He turned back to her. "Don't you want to go inside? You can show me where the phone is and sit down and rest."

"Well—" she glanced apprehensively at the house. "If you're going in too—"

He eyed her again. The night had stripped away the borderline adulthood of her eighteen years. She looked and sounded like a forlorn waif of a child. He thought she was about fifteen, the same age as his own daughter. His voice took on a paternal note as he said, "Oh yes, I'll go in with you."

She didn't look at Rollie, slumped against the railing with his eyes closed, as she went past him up the steps. The sergeant held the door for her, and for the last time she went into the house. She would remember it with horror; but at the moment, in his protective custody, it was less frightening than it would become in retrospect.

They crossed the dingy living room. She pointed out the phone in the dining room and sank onto the nearest chair.

"Are you going to get a doctor for Rollie?" she asked as the sergeant lifted the receiver.

"He the guy who got shot?"

"Yes."

"We'll get him one."

"Dr. Cramer knows the family," she said. "He was taking care of Mrs. Johnson."

"Okay, we'll try to get him." The sergeant dialed police headquarters.

Mandy, too numb to pay attention, heard only snatches of what he said. He needed more men, then something about women prisoners and herself—was he talking about policewomen?—a doctor, Dr. Cramer if they could reach him, not just for Rollie, he mentioned her. "The girl's in a state of shock," he said, which was an exaggeration. She was very tired and wet and dirty, but as soon as she found the energy to clean herself up . . .

Her eyes closed. The next thing she knew, the sergeant was shaking her gently by the shoulder. "Look, kid, I know you've just about had it, but you can't go to sleep on us now." He got her to her feet, his arm around her waist. "Come on in the other room and we'll find you a more comfortable place to sit. Lieutenant Bender's on his way and you'll have to give us some idea of what's been going on around here tonight."

She came awake with her story pouring out of her. "They killed Mrs. Johnson, the old lady who owns this house, and tried to pretend she was still alive. I don't know what they did with her body. Then, tonight, they tried to kill me. Their name is Avery. The daughter's been my pen pal for years but now they're calling each other by different names and—"

"Just a minute." He took her into the living room and settled her in an armchair. "There," he said. "You take it easy until the lieutenant gets here. Then you can tell us the whole story all at once."

He vanished outside. There were comings and goings for the next interval. The Averys, Janet still sobbing, were herded into the kitchen and left there under guard. Rollie, unconscious, or giving that appearance, was carried in and placed on the sofa. The phone rang. The sergeant answered it, talked briefly and then went out to the kitchen and put on a pot of coffee.

It was for her, Mandy gathered, and refrained from telling him that she hadn't yet acquired any great liking for it. He asked her where she lived. She explained that her parents were on a cruise and gave him her grandmother's address. She closed her eyes after that and fell asleep again, awaking a few minutes later to the sound of cars whipping up the driveway. Ambulance attendants appeared with a stretcher. Then a doctor came into the room. He gave Rollie a brief examination, supervised his removal from the sofa to the stretcher and went out to the ambulance with him.

A middle-aged policewoman appeared next, introduced herself as Mrs. Hodge and took charge of Mandy, who found herself being led upstairs to her room, stripped of her wet clothes and wrapped in her robe while a hot bath was being drawn for her.

At first glance she didn't recognize the bedraggled figure in the mirror as herself. How she looked didn't matter at the moment, though. She turned from the mirror and sat down on the bed. When the policewoman came back into the room tears were marking a path down her dirty scratched face.

"I keep thinking about being in this room earlier," she wept. "Mrs. Avery standing over the bed. She scared me to death. I pretended I was asleep but I was so scared I thought—"

"Well, try not to think about it," the policewoman said soothingly. "You come and have a nice hot bath and then we'll let the doctor take a look at you. Meanwhile, I'll lay out clean clothes and we'll get you a cup of coffee and you'll feel much better."

Mandy, under normal circumstances, wouldn't have allowed the policewoman to be in the bathroom with her. But she was past all sense of privacy. In a reversion to childhood she offered no protest as Mrs. Hodge scrubbed her and gave her a quick shampoo while she was still in the tub.

When she was back in her room and had put on underwear and her robe, Mrs. Hodge brought in the doctor, a white-haired man with a ruddy face.

"This is Dr. Cramer," she said. He smiled and nodded and opened his bag.

"Oh, you're Mrs. Johnson's—?" A thermometer thrust in her mouth cut off Mandy's question. The doctor took her pulse, listened to her heartbeat and dabbed an antiseptic solution on the worst of her cuts and scratches.

"I guess you'll do," he said. He sat back and looked at her with a professional eye. "The police want to ask you some questions. Do you feel up to it?"

"Yes, I'm all right. Just tired and sort of nerved up, I guess." Mandy sought to re-establish herself as an adult.

"Well, I'll tell them they can just hit the high spots tonight. What you need most, young lady, is about ten or twelve solid hours of sleep. How old are you?"

"Eighteen."

He closed his bag and got up to leave. Mandy said

quickly, "You've been taking care of Mrs. Johnson, the old lady who owns this house, haven't you, Doctor?"

"Mrs. Johnson?" He raised his bushy white eyebrows. "I have two Mrs. Johnsons for patients but neither one is an old lady or ever lived in this house. The last I knew it belonged to a Mrs. Gorman. She was an old lady and lived here for years. She died at the hospital last winter. But she wasn't one of my patients. As a matter of fact, I've never been in this house before."

"But—I was told—"

"Whatever you were told was wrong." He picked up his bag. "Good night. I'll tell them downstairs not to expect too much from you. Give me a call in the morning if there's anything more I can do for you."

He was gone, leaving Mandy looking after him in bewilderment. The old lady hadn't been his patient. . . .

She put on the blouse and skirt the policewoman handed her and let her brush her hair.

Cars came and went outside. Police officers moved from one room to another.

"They're searching the house," Mandy said.

"Yes, I guess so. What lovely hair you have, child. So thick and yet so fine and silky. It's still quite damp, though. I hope you won't catch a cold from it. It's too bad we don't have a hair drier handy."

Mandy didn't mention that Janet had one. She didn't want to use anything that belonged to her. Getting her hair dry didn't matter that much.

There was a knock on the door. A young policeman Mandy hadn't seen before stood in the doorway. "We've got coffee made and we sent out for hamburgers," he announced. "Lieutenant Bender says to tell you that they're ready downstairs."

"We'll be right down," Mrs. Hodge said.

Mandy stood up and went to the mirror, gathering her

hair into a ponytail. She secured it with a rubber band and then pinned it up on her head in a further assertion of adult status.

Her pallor startled her. The bruise and scratches on her face stood out against it. She had no way of concealing them, but she reached for her lipstick and made up her mouth.

"Shall we go down now?" she said.

The change in her appearance had its effect on the policewoman, shifting them from a mother-child relationship to more of an equal footing. "Whenever you're ready," she replied.

The living room seemed crowded with men. Mandy hesitated in the doorway, her eyes, darkly brilliant with a combination of fatigue and excitement, going from one to another. But when they stood up at her entrance she saw that there were only four; her friend the sergeant who was giving her a surprised glance as he mentally revised her age upward, the young policeman who had been sent to summon her and two men in plain clothes. They were all big men, though, tending to fill the room.

The sergeant performed introductions. "Lieutenant Bender, Detective Whitman, Officer Cawley. And by the way, my name's Garcia. I don't think I mentioned it before."

They were drinking coffee. They offered her the armchair she had sat in earlier and Officer Cawley brought in more coffee and hamburgers, Mrs. Hodge settling down in the background with hers.

Mandy said she wasn't hungry. The lieutenant, a youngish man but already bald, said, "See if you can't eat some of it, Miss O'Brien. It'll make you feel better."

He was smiling but firm. The girl felt that she couldn't swallow a mouthful, but with the first bite of her hamburger she discovered that she was hungry and ate every bit of it and drank her coffee.

She asked if they had got in touch with her grandmother. They hadn't been able to locate her yet. The Bangor police had reported that she wasn't home and that they were trying to find out where she had gone.

The lieutenant gave her a cigarette when she had finished eating. Then he pulled up a straight chair, straddled it and began, "Now, Miss O'Brien, I'm going to try to keep my questions down to a minimum for tonight; Dr. Cramer says that what you need more than anything else is to get to bed and get some sleep. But you must realize that we're completely at sea here. We've got that fellow one of our men shot under guard in the hospital. The others are still out in the kitchen, but they're just not talking. There are two cars outside that were rented from two different agencies in Syracuse. One of them was rented to Arthur Avery, the other to Roland Avery. They gave a Buffalo address, the one that shows on their driver's licenses. It's phony. We've already checked it with the Buffalo police and it doesn't exist. Before we take them to headquarters for questioning we should have some idea of who they are and what was going on here tonight. When you called the operator you said they—the Averys, I assume—were trying to kill you."

"Yes, they were," Mandy said.

"All right, let's start with who they are and what your connection with them is. Just the general outline for now. We'll fill it in later."

"Well, first of all, they're not from Buffalo," Mandy said. "They live in Bentonville, New York."

"Bentonville?" The lieutenant nodded to Sergeant Garcia, who immediately went to the phone in the dining room, and after a brief conversation came back and sat down again.

Mandy went on to her pen pal friendship with Janet Avery, the invitation to visit her, her arrival in Syracuse, the change in plans that had brought them to this house instead of to the Averys' in Bentonville.

Her voice shook slightly when the old lady came into her story. She paused, took a deep breath and said, "They killed her. I don't know how or when. They made me think she was still alive—I'd hear what I thought was her voice and there were lots of other things to make it seem real, like pretending that Dr. Cramer came every day—and it never crossed my mind that she wasn't up there in that horrible room."

Mandy shook her head ruefully. "What worried me most was that I thought they were trying to hasten her death by not giving her enough to eat. Perhaps that's what they did. Perhaps it was weeks ago."

"Why do you think they brought you into it?" Lieutenant Bender inquired.

Mandy looked at him in doubt. Then she said slowly, "The only thing I've thought of is that they needed a witness who'd say she was still alive and I guess I'd have been ready to swear to it on a stack of Bibles—the voice, you see, and all the rest of it."

She hesitated and then went on, "I suppose the picture changed for them somehow—it must have happened today very suddenly—and when they found out they didn't need me as a witness any more they decided to kill me. The change had something to do with the old lady's money, I think. I don't know what else it could be."

"Money?" Bender's glance sharpened.

"She had fifty thousand in cash, Janet said. They'd been looking for it here in the house, but it was somewhere else. They just got hold of it tonight. I heard them talking about it."

"Fifty thousand, you said?" The lieutenant looked thoughtful.

"Yes."

"Well, let it go for the moment. There's something else—" He stood up and went into the dining room.

Mandy heard a switch click and then a steady hum.

Lieutenant Bender came back and stood in the doorway. The hum continued, a sound she recognized but couldn't quite identify.

"What is it?" she asked.

He held up his hand. "Just listen."

A moment later she heard a familiar voice cry, "Evelyn! Janet! One of you come up here."

"A tape recorder." She looked at him with astonishment. "A tape recorder . . ."

17

It stood on the dining room table. "We found it in the back bedroom upstairs," the lieutenant said. "They used a lot of tapes but didn't put much on any of them. They're all labeled, though, with what the voice says, and they run for a couple of minutes, like the one you just heard, before the voice comes on. They didn't have it connected to a remote control switch so I would say that's why they left the first part blank. It gave them a chance to go upstairs, put a spool of tape on the recorder, and get back down with everyone present and accounted for before the voice started calling."

"I guess it worked out like that most of the time." Mandy stared as if hypnotized at the recorder. "But the old lady's voice—" She shivered. "How cold-blooded they were, planning her murder and getting it on tape to make use of it later."

The lieutenant pursed his mouth. "Who says it's her voice?"

"But—"

"Could be Mrs. Avery's or the daughter's. Wait a minute, though. Let's go back in the other room. Easier for Officer Cawley," he glanced at the young policeman who stood in the doorway with his notebook, "to take notes sitting down."

When they had resumed their places in the living room Lieutenant Bender continued, "It doesn't take a great actress to imitate an old woman's voice. It's just a high cracked falsetto."

"Mrs. Avery," Mandy said on a faraway note. "She mentioned something about being in a little theater group when she was young. . . ." She fell silent, sorting out all that had gone into her unquestioning acceptance of the old lady. "The nurse was just leaving, they said, the night we arrived. There was a car in the yard—"

"But you didn't see the nurse, did you?"

"No, I just heard the car drive away."

"Were they all here at the time?"

"Not Rollie. We had dropped him off outside of Syracuse."

"So he got here first—unless there's a fifth person involved. Has there been anyone else around?"

"No one at all." Mandy, still sorting out, added, "Phone calls, though, people asking how Mrs. Johnson was. I don't see how Mrs. Avery dared—"

She came to a halt again, thoughts, impressions jumbled together in her mind. She looked at the lieutenant and then at the others uncertainly. "Sunday," she said, "the day after I got here, Janet even took me upstairs to meet her grandmother. We were right outside the bedroom door. If I'd taken the lead and opened it—"

"But you didn't," Bender said. "They knew it was safe, that you wouldn't push your way into the sickroom of an old lady you'd never met. It was just a little act they threw in for good measure."

Sergeant Garcia put in a comment. "They sure went to a lot of trouble setting it up so you'd buy it," he said to Mandy.

"Well, I did," she replied. "I never once questioned it. It really bugs me—" she broke off in confusion remembering what her mother said about that expression and not using it in front of older people.

She stole a glance around the circle from under her lashes. No one looked disapproving. She went on hurriedly, "I feel like a fool when I think how I worried about her trays—"

"Well, let's get on to the old lady's money," the lieutenant said.

"All right." As Mandy leaned back in her chair bright lights in the barn caught her eye through the side window. The door stood open, but she couldn't see what was going on inside.

Bender waited a moment until her attention came back to him and then said, "We found a green plaid canvas bag in the Plymouth. Did you ever see it here in the house?"

"No, not that I remember."

"There was a hundred and fifty thousand cash in it."

"I don't understand that. Janet seemed to think it was only fifty thousand."

"Well, what we found, all in twenties and fifties, is three times—" He broke off as an officer came in from the kitchen, closing the door after him. "Yes, Webster?" he said.

"Nothing there, sir," the officer reported. "The ground's hard as a rock below where the digging stopped."

Digging. It could have only one connotation at this point.

The blood drained out of Mandy's face. They were looking for the old lady's body, had come across something that made them think it was buried nearby.

She waited until the officer left and then said to the lieutenant, "They kept the barn locked. Do you think they buried Mrs. Johnson out there?"

"I don't know much about her yet," Bender said. He ran his hand over his bald head. His glance weighed Mandy.

At last he said, "Well, I might as well give it to you straight, Miss O'Brien. The barn has a wood floor. It's been torn up in one corner and a hole dug underneath." He paused. "The hole is about the size and shape of a grave. A very deep grave. Deep enough for—"

"For two people?" Mandy felt faint. "For me and Mrs. Johnson?"

"We don't know who or what it was for yet so let's not

dwell on it." He eyed her with concern. "Are you all right? Would you like a drink of water?"

Mrs. Hodge started to rise and subsided as Mandy said quickly, "No, I'm okay." She sat up straight. "I'm fine. It was just that—"

"I know. Well, let's get back to Mrs. Johnson. Mrs. Avery was her adopted daughter, you said. She was bedridden and supposed to be dying. Did they say she was a widow?"

"Yes, but perhaps it wasn't true. Perhaps none of it was. Mrs. Avery lied about her living here all her married life and about being brought up here herself. Dr. Cramer said another old lady, a Mrs. Gorman, lived here for years and died last winter in the hospital."

"He say what she died of?" Bender inquired.

"No."

At a nod from him Sergeant Garcia went to the phone, came back and said, "Mrs. Gorman died of cancer."

"Oh." The lieutenant, frowning, got up from his chair and walked out into the hall, where he stood at the door for a moment surveying the floodlighted activities outside. When he returned to the room he said to the young police-man, "Cawley, make a note that we check with probate court in the morning and find out who inherited this house from Mrs. Gorman."

"Yes, sir."

"Tax collector's office might help," Detective Whitman suggested. He got to his feet. "I'd better see how things are going outside."

When he was gone Bender looked at Mandy. He wore a brooding expression. "I wonder if Mrs. Johnson ever existed," he said. "Or if she's what you might call the red herring in the case."

"What?" Mandy stared at him.

"So far, she's somebody's voice on a tape recorder, Miss O'Brien."

The concept of the old lady's nonexistence was too staggering for Mandy to absorb all at once. After a moment she said, "I have to think about it. I see what you mean, that the Averys could have made her up, but there were people who phoned to ask how she was—".

"Surely, Miss O'Brien, you know what number to dial to make your own phone ring? They had two phones to work with."

"But why should they have invented her?" Mandy asked. "What reason could they have had?"

"I don't know, so let's skip it for the moment. We've got enough background information now, I guess, for you to tell us what went on here tonight. Right from the beginning."

"Well, it began with the cat." She told them about it, the way it had been hanging around the house since her arrival, the Averys maintaining that it didn't belong to the old lady and Rollie threatening to kill it.

"It's outside now. It acts as if it belongs here," Sergeant Garcia interpolated. "Must have been Mrs. Gorman's. Maybe somebody took it in when she went to the hospital and it got away and came back here."

The sergeant was a cat lover, Mandy thought, but Lieutenant Bender seemed to consider its homeless plight an unnecessary digression. He shot an impatient glance at his subordinate as he said, "How did the cat come into it tonight, Miss O'Brien?"

She ignored his impatience. "The back bedroom must have been Mrs. Gorman's," she informed the sergeant. "When it got in tonight it ran straight up there."

She went on to what had followed: her pursuit and capture of the cat, her myriad anxieties about the old lady that had suddenly crystallized in the impulse to go into her room and take a look at her, the shock of finding it empty, her decision to get out of the house immediately and the setback Mr. and Mrs. Avery's arrival had given to her plans.

Bender interrupted her with questions when she came to what she had heard them say about her drink being drugged; and again when she brought in their talk about money; but she had been too frightened at the time and too much had happened afterward for her to remember very clearly what they had said about it.

She went on to her flight from the house, disrupted by the cat, the flash of lightning that had revealed her in the field. At this point she mentioned that the Averys had been calling each other by different names, but Bender, nodding thoughtfully, didn't pursue the subject. She had been prepared to bring in her own views on it but, instead, told them the rest of what had happened: her return to the house and phone call to the operator, her hiding on the roof and ultimate discovery, and her last wild flight that had ended with her being caught just as the police arrived.

"A couple of minutes more and it would have been too late." The lieutenant shook his head. "That was really quite a thing to have to go through."

"Not my idea of a pleasant evening." Mandy resorted to understatement, not wanting to lay stress on the fact that she had been reliving her ordeal in the telling of it. But she couldn't help adding, "It's not so great as a topic of conversation either. I'd just as soon talk about something else or let it all go till tomorrow. But where am I going to sleep tonight? I couldn't stay here. I want to get out of this house and never see it again." She looked at her watch. "It's almost quarter of two. Is there a hotel or motel in Noroton that will take me in at this hour?"

"Oh, you'll have no trouble at the Greenwood," Bender assured her. "Sergeant, will you call and get Miss O'Brien a room? And in the meantime, Mrs. Hodge, will you go upstairs and pack her things?"

"Yes, certainly, Lieutenant." The policewoman went up to Mandy's room.

Sergeant Garcia came back and announced that he had made a reservation for her.

"Good," she said, yawning openly. "I'm dead."

"Just a few more questions and I'll let you go," Bender said. "Although I wish we'd hear from Bangor first. Wouldn't you feel better if you could talk to your grandmother? Funny they haven't located her."

Mandy smiled suddenly, thinking of her energetic little grandmother. "She's always on the go, visiting people, dashing off here and there. No wonder they're having trouble finding her."

"We ought to hear from Bentonville too. I don't know what's keeping them."

"It's the middle of the night," the sergeant reminded him. "When people are in bed and asleep these things take more time."

"I suppose so," Bender conceded. He hitched his chair closer to Mandy's. "Miss O'Brien, we all know that everything that went on here tonight was a threat to your life, but was that threat ever put into words? Unless it was, you see, those people will deny that they meant to kill you; they'll say they just wanted to drug you and when that didn't work, use some other restraint while they made their getaway with the money. But if you heard them make a verbal threat on your life, it changes the whole picture."

"Well, Rollie said . . ." She told him what she had heard from the window, her voice fading a little at the memory of it as she repeated Rollie's words ". . . if she lives to tell her story."

"I guess that will do it." The lieutenant got to his feet. "Sergeant, have Whitman take those people in for questioning now. He can tell them that the charge will be conspiracy to murder for a start. God knows what we'll be adding to it before we're through."

The sergeant left. A few minutes later two cruisers drove out of the yard conveying the Averys to headquarters.

Their removal was a relief to Mandy. Ever since she had come downstairs she had been conscious of their presence in the kitchen behind the closed door. She could breathe more freely now that they were gone.

She sighed audibly. Her extreme pallor and the dark smudges under her eyes were outer signs of her bone-deep weariness.

Bender looked at her with compunction. "I've been pushing you too hard. You're about at the end of your rope, aren't you?"

"That's right," she said. "I really am."

"I'll have someone drive you and Mrs. Hodge to the hotel as soon as she finishes packing your things. She'll stay with you tonight. While we're waiting for her, though, let's just touch on what you said about those people using different names."

Sergeant Garcia, Mandy's self-appointed protector, was back in the room and moved restlessly. It was time the lieutenant stopped putting the poor kid through the jumps, he thought. The rest could wait until morning.

"They were calling Janet Barbara," Mandy informed Bender tiredly. "Mrs. Avery was Flo instead of Evelyn and so forth."

"And you'd never laid eyes on any of them until last Saturday."

"No, not until then."

Before the lieutenant could get in another question Mrs. Hodge came down the stairs with Mandy's suitcase in one hand and her raincoat bundled up in the other.

"I put all your wet things in your raincoat," she informed

the girl. "Although I'm afraid the skirt and blouse you had on are ruined."

"It doesn't matter. Thank you, Mrs. Hodge."

The telephone rang. Bender answered it. When he returned to the room his gaze settled on Mandy. "That was headquarters," he said. "They just got a report from the Bentonville police that the Averys, your pen pal and her parents, were home in bed and haven't been away all week." He paused. "Is that much of a surprise to you?"

"No, not now. After all, once I had a chance to think about the names. Even before tonight, though, in some subconscious way I—" She stopped short. "Oh, I don't know," she said next. "Maybe it's hindsight—except that almost as soon I walked into this house I began to get the feeling that something was very wrong."

"I should think so," the sergeant contributed. "Just the looks of it would be enough for me."

"Well, I felt that way too, but they kept offering explanations for it. In the future," she smiled at him wryly, "I'll listen to my instincts." She turned to the lieutenant. "What did the real Averys say?"

"They said they had a call Saturday morning that was supposed to be from one of your neighbors. The woman said that your mother had asked her to call and tell them you couldn't come. She said you'd been in a car accident the night before and were in the hospital and that your mother was with you and that was why she couldn't make the call herself. She said you weren't seriously hurt and that they would let you go home from the hospital the next day. Then, to keep the Averys from calling later in the day to ask how you were, the woman said your mother would be at the hospital until late that night and would call them the next morning. Very neat, wasn't it? Took the Averys right out of the picture."

"Unless they called the next morning before my parents

left on their cruise," Mandy said. "They wouldn't call that early, though. And by the time they did, my parents would be gone and there'd be no answer. But the Averys must have been wondering all week why they haven't heard anything."

Bender wasn't listening. He caught the sergeant's eye. "Thing's shaping up, don't you think?"

His subordinate nodded. "It sure is."

Bender got to his feet. "What's the phone number at your place in Maine?" he asked Mandy.

She gave it to him, adding, "But it's no use calling it. There's no one there. My parents won't be back until tomorrow night."

"Nevertheless, I think I'll try it." He went to the phone.

Sergeant Garcia, who had been so concerned a few minutes ago to get Mandy to her hotel, showed no disposition now to hurry her away.

Mandy herself had reached the stage of exhaustion where it was easier just to sit than to make any move at all.

The call went through quickly. She came out of her lethargy when she heard Bender speak to someone. Who was home? Had her parents got back a day early?

She jumped up and ran into the dining room. She wanted to snatch the phone out of the lieutenant's hand but had to hold back. He was listening to whoever was at the other end of the line. Then he said, "I see. You don't know when he'll be back. Well, this is Lieutenant Bender, Noroton Police Department, speaking, Mrs. O'Brien. Your daughter is here with me—"

"What?" From the middle of the room Mandy heard her mother's cry.

"Everything's all right. She's fine."

Mandy was beside him reaching for the receiver.

"Mother?" she said. "Mother—?"

"Oh, darling, it's you, it's really you. Oh, baby, dearest—"

Her mother's voice uttering endearments that came from

a heart almost breaking with love and pain and overwhelm-
ing relief was too much for Mandy. She burst into tears.
"Mommy," she sobbed. "Oh, Mommy, will you and Daddy
please come and get me right away? Please—"

She couldn't go on. The lieutenant took the receiver from
her.

Mrs. Hodge hurried into the room, put her arm around
her and led her back to her chair saying, "There, dear, there
now. Everything's going to be all right."

Mandy cried against her shoulder. Officer Cawley brought
a glass of water to her. The sergeant hovered helplessly.

When the lieutenant finished talking with her mother he
made another call. Mandy had herself under control again
by the time he came back into the room. He stood looking
down at her. His voice was gentle as he said, "Mandy, your
mother will take the first plane out of Bangor in the morning.
She'll be in Syracuse by midafternoon. Your father says that
you and he will plan to meet her plane."

"My father—?"

"I just talked to him. Your mother told me where to
reach him. He's at a motel in Syracuse and said to tell
you he'll be on his way here immediately. He went there
by plane yesterday afternoon and rented a car right away
so that he'd be ready to go anywhere at a moment's notice
to pay out the money and pick you up. Those people who
called themselves the Averys got the money from him tonight and had promised to release you within the next
twenty-four hours. It was ransom money, one hundred and
fifty thousand. You were kidnapped, Mandy, the minute
you stepped off the plane at Hancock Airport Saturday
night."

She got into pajamas at the hotel but insisted on waiting up for her father. She was asleep in a chair, Mrs. Hodge in attendance, when he arrived and didn't so much as stir when he carried her to her bed and drew the covers up over her. Standing beside the bed unable to take his eyes off her, drinking in the sight of her, this beloved daughter, restored to him against all odds, he broke down completely.

Mandy slept until one o'clock the next afternoon and when she woke up found both her parents keeping watch over her, her mother having arrived by chartered flight from Boston.

She flung herself into their arms.

Later that afternoon she spent several hours at the police station filling in her story and signing a statement, supplemented by her father's statement on his contacts with the kidnappers and payment of the ransom money.

Lieutenant Bender worked throughout the day, directing the activities of auxiliary police as well as regulars, and by evening felt that he had the main outlines of his case fairly complete.

A local reporter had got word of the kidnapping in time to include it in a news broadcast at noon. The chief of police released an official statement on it in midafternoon. Soon thereafter out-of-town reporters for all the news media began to arrive in Noroton, converging on the hotel in vain efforts to interview Mandy and her parents, who sought seclusion in their rooms, not ready yet to face the publicity that lay ahead.

A crowd began to collect outside the hotel and was so

dense when Bender stopped by on his way home that he had trouble forcing his way through it. He was recognized in the lobby and besieged by reporters, but was firm in his refusal to enlarge upon the brief statement he had given them earlier, asserting that any further information they received that night would have to come from the chief of police.

He shook them off at the elevator and rode up to the third floor, where there were policemen stationed outside the suite Mandy's father had taken and patrolling the corridor.

"Everything okay?" he said to the one at the door.

"Yes, sir."

"Good." He knocked and was admitted to the sitting room by Mandy's father.

He was off duty now after having been on since midnight the night before, grateful for the comfort of a big lounge chair and the drink offered him.

"It's been a day," he said, his glance drifting from one to the other, Mandy on the sofa beside her mother, Mr. O'Brien in another lounge chair opposite him.

His glance lingered longest on Mandy. He had no daughter of his own and found himself baffled by her transitions from young lady to child and back again. Tonight, her hair done up, wearing high heels and a trim dark dress, she was very much the young lady.

They talked for a few minutes about the family seeing the press in the morning and what should or shouldn't be said. When that was settled the lieutenant told them there was no reason why they couldn't leave on an afternoon plane. "I'm sure you want to get home," he added.

"Oh yes," Mrs. O'Brien said. "Mandy's grandmother is waiting for us at our cottage in Camden. We've talked to her two or three times today on the phone but it's not the same thing as getting back there with Mandy."

"No indeed." Bender took a sip of his drink—very good liquor it was, too, he thought—and said, "The Averys tried to call you but weren't able to since you're not taking any calls. They phoned headquarters just before I left. They'd like to drive up and see you tomorrow. They're pretty upset, of course, about the whole thing."

"I suppose we ought to at least—" Mr. O'Brien began and was checked by an imploring glance from Mandy. "Would you rather we went straight home, hon?"

"Much rather. Gran and everything. I just want to go home."

"Well, that's what we'll do then. I'll call the Averys in the morning and explain. We'll be meeting them later on, anyway, when we come back for the trial. How soon is it apt to come up, Lieutenant?"

"Sometime in the fall term. They'll be arraigned in municipal court tomorrow morning on charges of kidnapping and conspiracy to murder and bound over. You'll have plenty of notice, don't worry about that. There are sure to be various points that will have to be straightened out before then."

The talk went back and forth. Mandy sipped her Coke and listened. Bender accepted a refill; Mrs. O'Brien declined, saying with a smile, "I can feel the one I just had on top of a cocktail before dinner. I don't know how I'd react to another."

"I guess you're all in," the lieutenant said. "I told your husband I'd stop by and give you a rundown on this thing, but I'll try to make it short."

He glanced at Mandy. "I suppose you keep thinking of the people in that house as the Averys, but to keep the story straight, whenever I mention the name I mean the real Averys.

"The girl who posed as Janet Avery is really Barbara Gagnon; the so-called Rollie Avery is Regan Howell who's

been going out with the Gagnon girl off and on for the
past year. The older couple, man and wife, are Steve and
Florence Howell. Howell is Regan's uncle, his father's
younger brother. The father deserted when Regan was a
baby and was never heard from again. The mother seems to
have been something of a tramp herself. She dumped Regan
on the Howells when he was a little kid and when last
heard from, she was living with some man in Baltimore."

A father who deserted you and a mother who went off
with another man—Mandy couldn't imagine herself with
parents like that. Rollie—no, Regan Howell—hadn't had
much of a start in life. Not that it could even begin to
excuse what he had done—nothing could—but still—

It was funny how things got so mixed up. . . . She'd been
more than lucky herself in her parents. Was that why she
was forever feeling sorry for the wrong people?

"The Howells have been living in Rochester for about
twelve years now," the lieutenant continued, "but before that
Howell was something of a drifter and had a lot of different
jobs, mostly as a salesman. He's got a record in Albany and
two or three other places. Stole five hundred dollars from
one firm he worked for and got off with a suspended sentence. Did ninety days for getting mixed up in a car theft
and a couple of other things like that. Nothing big, ever,
you see, perhaps because nothing big ever offered itself. Until last spring.

"Regan's been attending the state teacher's college in
Bentonville, not because he wanted to be a teacher but because he knew he'd better get some kind of an education
and that was the only kind he could afford.

"He's got a juvenile court record. Truancy in his elemen-
tary school days and a particularly ugly little incident when
he was eleven years old. He tied a neighbor's child, a nine-
year-old girl to a tree, hanged her cat right in front of her
and frightened her half to death with threats to cut her up

with his jackknife. When he was brought into juvenile court the girl's parents didn't want to press their complaint and it was dropped."

Mandy's mother reached for her hand suddenly and held it tight for a moment before she released it.

"He was mixed up in some pretty vicious school vandalism when he was fifteen and was put on probation. There's no further record on him.

"His school record has been spotty all along. Considered very bright but did good work only when he felt like it. Dropped out of college after his freshman year, stayed out a year and then went back. Barely maintained passing marks but had no plans to take summer courses until the kidnapping project began to develop among the three of them."

"Wasn't Barbara Gagnon in on it all along?" Mandy's father asked. "What's her background?"

"Well . . ." Bender shrugged. "About what you'd expect. The type that never does much in school, starts running around with boys before reaching the teens, poor home background with very little supervision from the parents. She did finish high school, although she was in the bottom third of her class. This was in Schenectady where she grew up. She's twenty-one, almost twenty-two, by the way. She left home after high school and began sharing cheap furnished apartments with other girls like herself. Worked in different stores as a salesgirl, went to a modeling school and when that didn't pan out, she left Schenectady and eventually ended up in Bentonville as a waitress in a diner. That's where she met young Howell last fall. She lost that job and then worked in a bakery up until two weeks ago when they got the kidnapping project all set up and she and the older couple took over the house. She told them at the bakery that she was going to try her luck in New York City;

the Howells told their neighbors in Rochester that they were going on a vacation."

Barbara Gagnon hadn't had a very good start in life either, Mandy reflected.

"Regan Howell had to stay in Bentonville to finish up the course he was taking. He attended both sessions of summer school. The whole plan, you see, revolved around his keeping in close contact with Janet Avery.

"He roomed with two elderly women next door to her. He'd been there all year and had got to know Janet pretty well. He didn't take her out on dates—after all, she was still in high school, with a different circle of friends—but they were friendly, he has a Volks and he'd drop her off at school in the morning and things like that. Mrs. Avery would invite him to dinner occasionally. He was always on his best behavior and she felt sorry for him, she says, not having much money and eating in cheap restaurants all the time."

The lieutenant looked at Mandy and said, "Janet Avery thinks it was around the first of May that you made a definite commitment to visit her in August. Is that about right?"

"Yes."

"Well, Janet seems to be one of these kids who's ready to take people into her confidence at the drop of a hat. So, naturally, she was bubbling over with excitement about meeting her pen pal at last, and told Regan Howell all about you. She showed him your picture and snapshots of your home in Connecticut and your summer place in Maine and gave him all kinds of information about you. She admits she did a lot of bragging about the kind of business your father owned, and how much money he had and how you went to a select private school and all that. She feels terrible about it now but at least she's honest, she didn't try to cover any of it up when she was questioned today. She realizes, looking back now, that Regan Howell was doing a lot of pumping, too, and that he kept seeking her out all summer. When the date for your visit was set she told him all about it, of course, what time your plane got in, how long you were going to stay, the whole works. So, just as she says, everything does go back to her."

"No, it goes back to me nine years ago," Mandy's mother said, turning anguished eyes on her daughter. "It was I, not your father or anyone else, who encouraged you to make Janet Avery your pen pal, just because I liked her mother so much the one time we met. Did you think of that, darling, while you were going through that awful nightmare last night?"

"Of course not," Mandy said loyally, "and you mustn't either. How could you ever have dreamed nine years ago—"

"I've thought of nothing else since that call came Saturday night. I answered the phone—did I tell you that?—and it was just a man's voice asking for your father. I put him on and he couldn't believe it at first, the man telling him you were kidnapped and that we must say nothing about it to anyone if we ever wanted to see you alive again. Then there were the instructions for me to call the Averys the next morning and tell them we were bringing you home from the hospital that day. And the second call Monday night from the man about your father going to a certain motel in Syracuse Tuesday—was it only yesterday?—with the money. They'd even made a reservation for him. I don't know how we lived through it—" she broke down in tears.

Mandy put both arms around her. "Don't, Mother. I'm here, I'm safe, it's all over."

"I thought I'd die Monday when a beautiful bouquet of flowers came for you from Janet Avery with a cheerful little message on the card. I thought I'd die—"

Mandy pressed her cheek against her mother's. "It's over, darling. It's over."

"Imagine your having to comfort me after what you went through yourself." Mrs. O'Brien took out a handkerchief and dried her eyes. "I'm sorry," she said to her husband and Bender.

"Don't give it a thought," the lieutenant said. "You've had plenty to cry about. It's going to take time to get over it."

"That's right." Mandy's father leaned forward and patted his wife's shoulder. "Just get it out of your system, Ruth, any way you can."

She gave him a watery smile. "I'm all right now, dear."

"Good." Mr. O'Brien settled back in his chair. "Let's hear the rest of the story, Lieutenant."

"The rest of it comes mostly from Barbara Gagnon," Bender said. "She's made a full confession and will be a witness for the prosecution at the trial."

"And get a lesser sentence for turning state's evidence?" Mandy's father inquired.

"That isn't up to me to say. All I know is, there have been some changes in the statutes on kidnapping this year." Bender's voice took on a neutral tone.

"But it's a Federal offense. Doesn't the FBI come into it?"

"No. We had an agent in this afternoon but it was just for the record, you might say. Mandy wasn't taken across a state line, you see; it's the state of New York that will indict and try these people. Well, to get on with the story: Barbara Gagnon fell hard for young Howell, but he was less interested, it seems, and just dated her off and on. She makes no bones about the kind of relationship they had, though. In the middle of the winter when the girl she was sharing an apartment with left, she asked Regan to move in with her. He didn't go for that, didn't want to get that involved, I guess, and more or less dropped her until about the middle of May.

"She's been thinking it over and has figured it out that what brought him back was the fact that in a very superficial way she bears a resemblance to Janet Avery. Sergeant Garcia, who went to Bentonville today, noticed it right off.

They both have blond hair and blue eyes—Barbara bleaches her hair but says she's sort of blond anyway—and they're about the same height and general build and have more or less average features with nothing distinctive about either of them.

"A couple of weeks after Howell began dating her again, he started to feel her out on the kidnapping plot along the lines of how would you like to make twenty thousand bucks, very little risk in it, and so forth. She wasn't hard to sell on it, I'd say, although she swears that not a word was said about murder being part of it until after the kidnapping took place. They told her it would have to end that way the night Regan Howell took Mandy to the drive-in. According to her, she wanted to back out then, but the older couple told her it was too late for that and made threats about what they'd do to her if she tried it."

"Did you believe that?" Mandy's father inquired.

"No, not really. They may not have spelled it out for her ahead of time, but how could she help realizing that they couldn't let your daughter go? It's not as if she were a young child who wouldn't be able to give any information about them."

That was the specter that had haunted Mandy's father from the moment of his first contact with the kidnappers: she would be able to tell too much if they let her go. Flying to Connecticut to get the ransom money, talking to the man who made the phone calls, trying to reassure and comfort his wife, flying to Syracuse, waiting for the phone to ring in his motel room, whatever he had done through the agonizing days and nights, that was the specter that had never left him.

Bender continued, "When the date for Mandy's visit was set young Howell had his aunt come to Bentonville, not to meet Janet Avery but to get a good look at her. Then Mrs. Howell went to work on Barbara. At one time, it seems, she'd had a few small parts on the stage and had acquired some skill in using makeup. She had Barbara tone down the bleach job on her hair and took her to a hairdresser to get the same kind of haircut that Janet Avery had. She reshaped Barbara's eyebrows and generally did everything she could to heighten the resemblance between the two of them. Barbara's clothes were too flashy to suit them, but they couldn't afford to buy her a new wardrobe.

"They didn't have much money, Barbara says. Regan Howell got a part-time job this summer and Mrs. Howell held a full-time one for a couple of months. Her husband borrowed on his life insurance and they scraped around to get the money together for expenses. They'd checked your financial standing, Mr. O'Brien, and Steve Howell then made a quick trip to Connecticut to pick up whatever additional information he could that would help them to set the ransom figure.

"It was Regan who invented the grandmother at death's door and after that they started spending their weekends scouting around for a suitable locale and house. They made a list of their requirements, Barbara says. The house had to be at least a hundred miles away from their home territory in Rochester and another hundred miles away from Bentonville. They sat down with a map and hit on an area that would be within twenty to thirty miles north or southeast of Watertown. The house had to be available for short-term rental, preferably furnished, and in an isolated spot. They decided that what they had to have was a fairly large rambling old house with a bedroom off by itself that they could say was the old lady's. It took them until the middle of July to find one that met their requirements.

"We've talked to the real estate agent who rented the place to them. He's handling it for Mrs. Gorman's two nieces who live in Binghamton. He says they took everything they wanted from the house and decided to leave the rest of the

furniture there for the time being to make it look more pre-
sentable. He hasn't had a single offer for it since he listed it
six months ago. We haven't asked him to make an identifica-
tion yet, but from his description, it was Mrs. Howell, calling
herself Mrs. Johnson, who rented it from him with a story
about an invalid mother who needed absolute quiet out in
the country. He contacted the heirs and found them agree-
able to renting it for any figure that wouldn't involve them
in repairs or redecorating.

"He asked for three months' rent in advance. Mrs. Howell
paid it, took possession of the house August 15 and had the
utilities connected the same day."

The lieutenant continued, "Barbara Gagnon says they all
pitched in to clean the place up, but except for buying a
cheap set of dishes and a few other things, they didn't spend
much to make it look lived in. Mrs. Howell brought her own
bed linens and cooking utensils. The tape recorder belonged
to Regan. She made the recordings after she got there with
the others listening downstairs to see if her voice sounded
right. They were all set then except to get in all the practice
they could in calling each other by their new names. They'd
been doing it all summer so there'd be no slipups."

Mandy eyed him soberly. "They went to a lot of trouble.
I don't see why they didn't just drive up some country road
the night I arrived and kill me right away. They could still
have collected the ransom. My father didn't know if I were
alive or dead last night when he left the money for them in
that cemetery in Cicero."

"If they'd been professional criminals that's what they
probably would have done," Bender said. "But cold-blooded
murder, particularly when it's being committed for the first
time, is a formidable crime, even to people like the Howells.
They counted on it that your father wouldn't go to the police, but if he did, or if anything else went wrong, at least
they wouldn't have to face a murder charge as long as they

could produce you alive and unharmed. Once they got their hands on the ransom money it was a different situation, of course. They were ready to take any risks then."

He went back to the mainstream of the story. "The day before you were due to arrive they went to Syracuse and rented two cars under their assumed names, giving the phony Buffalo address they had used when they took out drivers' licenses there as Arthur and Roland Avery. Young Howell didn't pick up his rented car until the next day. When he separated from the rest of you in Syracuse, Mandy, he went on to the house in his own car to pretend it was the nurse leaving. He had plenty of time to get there first while you were all stopping at a restaurant. Barbara says that was where Steve Howell made his first phone call to your father."

Mandy looked at her parents. It didn't bear thinking of that while she sat in the restaurant booth feeling no emotion deeper than dismay and doubt as to how successful her visit was going to be, her father and mother were being hit with the news that she had been kidnapped.

Bender continued, "Regan Howell kept his car in Syracuse and switched back and forth when he went to Bentonville. He slept in his room there every night and took an exam Monday morning at the college. He wanted to keep in touch with what was going on at the Averys' and to show himself in Bentonville as much as he could to build up an alibi, knowing that as a friend of Janet's, he'd be questioned when the case broke out in the open. They had every last detail figured out; they didn't overlook a thing."

"They took a lot of chances with me, though," Mandy said slowly. "I went to church in Noroton, swimming at Watson's Pond, out riding and to dinner and any number of things. They let me run around loose the whole time."

"You didn't have half the freedom you thought you had," Bender informed her. "You were always among strangers

away from the house and constantly being policed, Barbara
says. You didn't even have freedom of movement on the second floor. Whenever you went upstairs someone went up
after you in case you got too curious about the old lady in
the back bedroom. No," he shook his head, "they weren't
taking any great chances with you. The whole setup was a
lot easier for them than if they'd tied you up and kept you
under guard twenty-four hours a day. According to Barbara,
they didn't think they had the manpower for it. Half the
time young Howell couldn't be there at all and I doubt
that they looked for much help from Barbara herself."

"No, they didn't," Mandy said, giving it thought. "I don't
think they trusted her."

"That's what I mean," Bender said. "There was just the
older couple. Over a three-day stretch they'd have to allow
time to eat and sleep and all that routine as well as needing
some freedom of their own to negotiate the ransom. They
were so cautious that Steve Howell drove almost to Syracuse
Monday night to make the second phone call to your father;
and last night it took two of them to collect the money, one
to keep a lookout at the wheel of the car and the other to
pick it up. They took all this into consideration, Barbara
says, and decided that the easier way was to keep you from
knowing what your position was."

"But it didn't take care of the unforeseen," Mandy said.
"Like the cat."

"Something equally unforeseen might have come up if
they'd had you tied hand and foot in one of the bedrooms,"
the lieutenant pointed out. "People have been known to escape from that kind of a situation." He smiled at her. "Just
last night you showed what you could do when you had
to."

His smile went to her parents. "You must be proud of
her."

"Proud's not a big enough word," her father said.

"Fast-foot Fran, that's me," Mandy said turning aside their praise. And then, "Is the cat still out there, Lieutenant? I don't want it to be left on its own."

"Sergeant Garcia fed it today and says he's going to take it home with him as soon as he's made friends with it." Bender stood up to leave. "Well, that's about it for the present, I guess. We'll be in touch with you as different things come up."

"Aren't you leaving something out, Lieutenant?" There was no lightness now in Mandy's tone. "The grave in the barn that was too deep just for me."

"Oh, darling," her mother protested.

"I'd much rather know everything," Mandy told her. "Much rather."

She went on looking at Bender. "When we talked about it last night it seemed that it was for the old lady too. But she didn't exist."

"We've had some thoughts on it," Bender admitted. "Not subject to proof."

"Barbara Gagnon?" Mandy persisted.

"We think so. Just guesswork. But look at the ransom money. Divided by three it comes out nice and even at fifty thousand apiece. The Howells set the figure and they're what you might call a closed corporation, with Barbara the complete outsider bringing nothing to their project but her superficial resemblance to Janet Avery. They must have looked on her from the beginning as a weak link—quite rightly, too, considering that we had very little trouble getting a full confession from her, once we separated her from them. They couldn't ever have felt safe if they let her go her way with her share of the money after they'd killed you. Putting it all together we're inclined to think that once you were taken care of, her time was up too. Not that we could ever prove it or would even try to, but the grave's too deep to make sense otherwise."

"God, what people," Mandy's father said. "God . . ."

"It takes all kinds, they say. Well, I'll see you in the morning before you leave." Bender headed for the door. "Good night and thanks for the drinks."

Not long after he left they all went to bed and Mandy discovered presently that she didn't want to put her light out. Her parents were just across the sitting room—she could hear them talking to each other—but, still, she didn't want to put her light out.

She puttered around her room and brushed her hair twice as long as she usually did. For the first time that she could ever remember she was afraid of the dark.

Her parents' light went out. Her mother called, "Want me to come and tuck you in?"

"I thought maybe I'd do that for you," Mandy replied, and went across the sitting room to their bedroom.

Her father turned on the light beside the double bed and looked at her in her short pajamas, barefooted, with her hair loose. He smiled. "All right, climb in with us. It's been a good many years since you have. Crack of dawn used to be your favorite time."

"It wasn't that bad," Mandy said, climbing over the foot of the bed. She gave a small sigh of content as she crawled in between them. "Here we are, all in a row, O'Briens, Incorporated. What does incorporated mean, Dad?"

"It's a long story. Let's just call it an association. Or do you want me to go into its legal status as separate from the individual or individuals forming it?"

"Let's skip it." Mandy spoke in a bright voice, but her parents caught the brittle note in it and exchanged a glance over her head. Then her father sat up and said, "You know, I've got a feeling that you girls are about to start on a bedtime chat and you're going to have to count me out. Would you mind, Mandy, if I slept in your bed and let you sleep here with your mother?"

"No, I wouldn't mind," she said magnanimously.

"It's a deal." He kissed them both good night and went off to her room.

"Will you turn out the light now?" her mother said.

Mandy turned it out. With her mother beside her the dark held no terrors.

They talked about buying a present for Gran tomorrow between planes in Boston and went on to what kind of a dress Mrs. O'Brien should get for the company's anniversary dinner next month. Mandy relaxed and began to get drowsy. At last she said, "I wish I didn't ever have to meet Janet Avery."

"I don't see how you can avoid it at the trial."

"I'll feel funny. I'll keep getting her mixed up in my mind with Barbara Gagnon. It's not fair to Janet, I know, but I doubt that I'll ever feel the same toward her again. I don't even want to write to her any more, but I don't want to hurt her feelings either."

"Taper it off," her mother counseled. "You'll both be in college and have new interests."

Mandy yawned. "Don't you think pen pal friendships begin to look a little retarded, anyway, when people start going to college?"

"Depends on how you feel about them, I guess."

Mandy yawned again. "Before you go to sleep, there's one last thing," her mother said.

"Yes?"

"Don't let your own children have pen pals, will you?"

"No, Mother. As a matter of fact, I'll beat their little brains out if they even mention the word."

"That's not a nice expression, darling."

"Pen pals," said Mandy, "aren't so nice either."

"Go to sleep," her mother said.